Betty

By Gary Delainey and Gerry Rasmussen.

BLUEFIELD ❧ BOOKS

Betty copyright © 1999 NEA, Inc. All rights reserved.

Betty is syndicated internationally by NEA, Inc., and can be visited on the web at www.comics.com

Betty is published by Bluefield Books
Gr. 12, C. 9, RR 1, Winlaw, B.C., Canada V0G 2J0
1-800-296-6955

ISBN 1-894404-01-7

Canadian Cataloguing in Publication Data

Delainey, Gary, 1956-
Betty

ISBN 1-894404-01-7
I. Rasmussen, Gerry, 1956- II. Title.
PN6734.B47D44 1999   741.5'971   C99-910769-0

Printed in Canada on recycled paper

For our parents and to our children

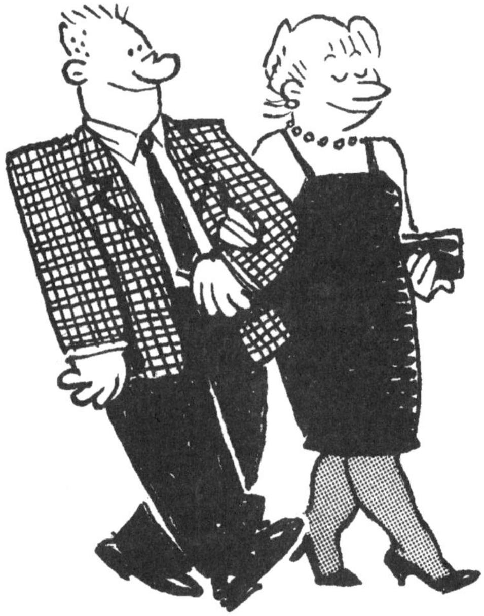

Betty
By Delainey and Rasmussen.
THERE'S SOMETHING INTERESTING...
A SCIENTIST IS DEVELOPING A COMPUTER YOU WEAR LIKE CLOTHING
WITH IT, THE WEARER WILL BE ABLE TO FILTER OUT INTRUSIVE NOISES AND SIGHTS THAT BOMBARD US REGULARLY
I WONDER WHAT THAT WOULD BE LIKE...
...TO ONLY SEE WHAT YOU WANT TO SEE, TO ONLY HEAR WHAT YOU WANT TO HEAR
"I SAID–"
WHAT? WERE YOU TALKING TO ME?
Delainey & Rasmussen

Betty
By Delainey and Rasmussen
TODAY ON POOLS, PATIOS AND PERGOLAS, WE'RE GOING TO LOOK AT THIS BEAUTIFUL BEACHSIDE GARDEN POOL COMPLETE WITH POOL HOUSE, KOI POND AND WATERFALL...
WELCOME TO HOUSE BEAUTIFUL. TODAY WE VISIT THE FULLY RESTORED 18th CENTURY PLANTATION HOUSE OF
CHAMPAGNE WISHES AND CAVIAR DREAMS...
ON FABULOUS RESORTS. LET'S VISIT...
GREAT CASTLES OF EUROPE...
FRESH MAINE LOBSTER WITH SWEET CORN, IT'S A GOOD THING!
WHATCHA WATCHING?
NVTV
Delainey & Rasmussen

7

Strip 1:

Panel 1: ZZZZZZ ZZZ

Panel 2: HEY! IS THAT A SILHOUETTE OF ME? — YEAH

Panel 3: I TOOK A PHOTO OF YOU AND DARKENED EVERYTHING EXCEPT THE DIAMOND IN YOUR ENGAGEMENT RING, JUST LIKE IN THOSE COOL DEBEERS ADS

Panel 4: EXCEPT NOW THAT I'VE PRINTED IT OUT I CAN'T FIND THE DIAMOND

Panel 5: THERE IT IS! —NOPE THAT'S A MOLECULE OF WHITE PAPER...

Strip 2:

Panel 4: BE HONEST. FOR YOU, THE WHOLE EVENING, NICE AS IT WAS, WAS MERELY A PRELUDE TO SLAPPING DOWN YOUR NEW NATIONAL HOCKEY LEAGUE MASTERCARD, WASN'T IT?

Strip 3:

Panel 1: I'M INPUTTING MY COLLECTION OF RECIPES FROM MY MOM, MY GRAMMA AND MY AUNTS INTO THE COMPUTER

Panel 2: THE EASY PART IS PUTTING IN THE INGREDIENTS AND THE INSTRUCTIONS — CLICK CLICKA CLICK

Panel 3: THE HARD PART IS CONVEYING THE LOVE OF THE WOMEN WHO PREPARED THEM DAY AFTER DAY

Panel 4: THANKS, BUT I DON'T THINK CLIPART IS THE ANSWER

SEE, FOR MOM'S MEATLOAF RECIPE, I'VE GOT A PICTURE OF HER AND DAD IN FRONT OF THEIR FIRST HOUSE
FOR GRAMMA'S APPLE CRISP— A PICTURE OF HER IN HER GARDEN
AND FOR AUNT SADIE'S CREAM MASHED POTATOES—
WELL, ALL I HAVE OF AUNT SADIE IS THIS PICTURE OF HER ON THE BEACH...
VERY EFFECTIVE. IT'D ALSO WORK FOR RICE PUDDING

WOW!
MY GREAT AUNT MILDRED'S RECIPE FOR SPAGHETTI SAUCE — SEE, THERE'S AN ACTUAL SAUCE STAIN ON THE RECIPE CARD!
COOL
TOO MUCH SALT, NOT ENOUGH GARLIC

NOT WATCHING TV?
NO, I'M LOOKING AT SOME HOLIDAY BROCHURES FOR OUR SUMMER VACATION
RAILWAY VACATIONS?
YEAH, LIKE THIS ONE— CLEAR ACROSS CANADA!
ARE YOU SERIOUS? DO YOU KNOW WHAT THAT'D BE LIKE? SITTING AROUND FOR DAYS, BROKEN ONLY BY MEALS AND SLEEP
THEN AGAIN, I FORGET WHO I'M TALKING TO
HEY!

Betty
By Delainey and Rasmussen.
...SIMPLY PUT, RAG ROLLING IS A PAINT FINISHING TECHNIQUE WHEREBY PART OF AN OUTER LAYER IS REMOVED WITH A CRUMPLED RAG TO ALLOW THE BASE COAT TO SHOW THROUGH — WITH STRIKING RESULTS!
REMEMBER THOUGH, THE SECRET IS PRACTICE, PRACTICE, PRACTICE!
NO RAG ROLLING PRACTICE IN THE ROAD GRIME!!
Delainey&Rasmussen

I DON'T GET IT
JUST HOW AM I SUPPOSED TO RELATE TO A DITSY, RAIL-THIN, MINISKIRT-WEARING LAWYER?
OH, WAIT...
HA-HA-HA HAHA
MIND YOU, IT IS FUNNY WHEN A DITSY, MINISKIRT-WEARING LAWYER GETS CREAMED IN A REVOLVING DOOR!

PERSONALLY, I THINK THE COURAGE SHE SHOWS BY WEARING A MINISKIRT MAKES ALLY McBEAL A FINE ROLE MODEL
WHAT?
SHE'S NOT INTIMIDATED BY THE CURRENT BIAS AGAINST CAPABLE WOMEN LOOKING FEMININE
THE LAST TIME YOU MADE THAT ARGUMENT WAS AFTER 'BATMAN RETURNS' AND YOU WERE TRYING TO GET ME INTO A LEATHER CAT SUIT
IT'S STILL A GOOD CHOICE. THEY'RE NEVER OUT OF FASHION

DO YOU WATCH ALLY McBEAL?
SURE
REALLY? HOW? IT'S SO CONTRIVED, SO FALSE, SO SMUG...
THAT'S WHAT I LIKE ABOUT IT
WHEN I WANT REAL, GENUINE AND SINCERE, I TURN OFF THE TV AND WATCH THE FISH TANK

WHY CAN'T THERE BE TV SHOWS ABOUT WOMEN LIKE US?
US?
YEAH, WHY ALWAYS YOUNG, SKINNY, HIGH-STRUNG DOCTORS, LAWYERS OR COPS?
WHY NOT REAL, EVERYDAY WOMEN?
YOU'D WATCH THAT?
UM... ..I... MIGHT...
YOU'RE SUCH A LIAR! I KNOW YOU; YOU CAN'T EVEN BE BOTHERED TO WATCH YOUR OWN HOME VIDEOS
DER.

BEA—ARE YOU DRESSED LIKE ALLY McBEAL?
WHO?
SHE'S ON TV...
NEVER HEARD OF HER
BUT IF SHE, LIKE ME, JUST TRIED A CHEAP DEPILATORY CAUSING HER TO SCREAM AT THE LIGHTEST TOUCH OF FABRIC ON HER LEGS, THEN SHE HAS MY SYMPATHY
DER.

HA HA HAW HEE HEE
WE'RE TAKING A LITTLE TIME OUT FOR SOME "DILBERT LAUGH THERAPY"
READ THAT ONE
YES, IT'S PAINFULLY TRUE, BUT CAN YOU ELABORATE ON WHY IT'S FUNNY?
BEA, MORE 'LAUGH,' LESS 'THERAPY'

Strip 1:
- "DOING REPAIRS, BEA?" "NOPE"
- "I'VE STOPPED USING A PURSE AND STARTED USING A TOOLBELT"
- "IT FREES UP MY HANDS, IT DOESN'T WEAR OUT AND IT'S GOT MORE POCKETS AND COMPARTMENTS"
- "AND THE HAMMER?" "EXACTLY! TRY CARRYING ONE OF THESE BAD BOYS IN A PURSE!"

Strip 2:
- "HEY! 'THE 7 HABITS OF HIGHLY EFFECTIVE PEOPLE'" "GOOD BOOK!" "SUBTITLED 'RESTORING THE CHARACTER ETHIC'"
- "OF COURSE I BOUGHT MINE IN FIRST EDITION HARDCOVER IN 1990 — BEFORE THERE WAS ALL THE 'PRAISE FOR...' PAGES IN FRONT OF THE BOOK, BEFORE IT HAD '#1 NATIONAL BESTSELLER' AND 'OVER 10 MILLION SOLD' ON ITS COVER"
- "AND BEFORE IT SHOWED UP ON OPRAH!"
- "I GUESS WHAT I'M SAYING IS, I OUGHT TO READ IT AGAIN"

Strip 3:
- "THIS IS A REALLY GOOD BOOK" "IT'S A CLASSIC OF THE SUCCESS GENRE"
- "IT BOGGLES THE MIND"
- "IF I'D READ THIS WHEN IT FIRST CAME OUT, I WOULD'VE BEEN HIGHLY EFFECTIVE FOR THE PAST EIGHT YEARS" "YEAH, RIGHT"
- "?" "YOU'RE NEW TO THE SUCCESS GENRE, AREN'T YOU?"

Betty
By Delainey and Rasmussen.
I THOUGHT YOU HAD AN APPOINTMENT AT THE CHIROPRACTOR
AFTER THE BUS RIDE, IT WASN'T NECESSARY
Delainey & Rasmussen

MY HUSBAND WANTS TO SPEND OUR FAMILY VACATION CROSSING CANADA BY TRAIN
JOHN WANTS TO GO ON A WALKING TOUR OF SCOTLAND DISTILLERIES
THE TROUBLE IS HE'S SO EXCITED ABOUT IT THAT I MIGHT HAVE TO GIVE IN AND GO
YEAH, I KNOW WHAT YOU MEAN
THEY NEVER REALLY STOP BEING LITTLE BOYS, DO THEY?
NOPE
AND YET THEY "WEAR THE PANTS"
TRUE,...WITH A SLINGSHOT IN ONE BACK POCKET AND A ROLLED-UP COMIC IN THE OTHER

SHAKES
IN LOV
THERE YOU GO— GETTING SPRITZED AT THE PERFUME COUNTER BEFORE A MOVIE: THE UPSIDE

THERE! FINALLY IT'S READY!
NEVER ORDER CAFÉ AU LAIT FROM SOMEONE WHO PRONOUNCES IT CAFÉ AU LATE
YOU SHOULD'VE ORDERED 'EXPRESSO.' I GOT MINE RIGHT AWAY

16

DER
WELL, IT HAD TO HAPPEN SOONER OR LATER
YEP
THE YOUNGER GENERATION HAS FINALLY FOUND A WAY TO REALLY BUG US
THEY'VE BECOME OUR PARENTS

THE NEW GENERATION IS REBELLING AGAINST US LIKE WE REBELLED AGAINST OUR PARENTS
CHECK
AND THEIR WAY OF REBELLING IS TO BE LIKE OUR PARENTS— DRINKING COCKTAILS, WEARING TAILORED GOWNS, LISTENING TO LOUNGE MUSIC
RIGHT
'GRUNGE' DIDN'T DO IT—BUT THIS... THIS REALLY HURTS
AND THEY MAKE IT LOOK LIKE SUCH FUN, TOO
DER

YEP, THEY'VE REALLY DONE IT THIS TIME
YEP
BY BECOMING LIKE OUR PARENTS, THE YOUNGER GENERATION HAS PAINTED US INTO A CORNER
YEP
DER
IF WE IGNORE THEM, WE MISS OUT ON THE FUN. IF WE JOIN THEM, WE ARE UNDERMINING OUR OWN REBELLION AGAINST OUR PARENTS
RIGHT
MAYBE IF WE BECAME LIKE THEIR PARENTS, THAT WOULD FIX 'EM
ALEX, OUR GENERATION IS THEIR PARENTS

THIS 'FIFTIES RETRO LOUNGE THING' REALLY BUGS YOU?
YEAH
FOR THE FIRST TIME, I WANT TO JOIN A FASHION TREND, BUT I CAN'T
SUDDENLY I FEEL OLD
I SAY LET THE YOUNGSTERS HAVE THEIR FASHION— IT'S OUR GENERATION THAT RULES THE WORLD
BETTY, DID YOU JUST SAY THE WORD "YOUNGSTERS"?!
OMIGOSH! I DID

SO THAT'S IT THEN, WE'RE OUT OF THE FASHION LOOP
GUESS SO
WE'RE STUCK LOOKING LIKE WHO WE ARE NOW FOR THE REST OF OUR LIVES
YOU KNOW, THERE'S A NASTY SIDE TO FASHION THAT I'M JUST BEGINNING TO COMPREHEND

SORRY, I DON'T BUY IT—
YOU DON'T GET THE MUNCHIES BECAUSE YOU'RE WEARING A HEMP SHIRT!

WHAT'S THAT?
IT'S CORE STABILIZATION. IT'S VERY DIFFICULT
IT DOESN'T LOOK TOO DIFFICULT, MIND IF I TRY?
BE MY GUEST
SEE? NO SWEAT
MY MISTAKE– APPARENTLY YOUR CORE IS SELF-STABILIZING

MOM, CAN I PAINT MY ROOM?
SURE, WHY NOT?
IT'S YOUR ROOM AFTERALL
GREAT! I'LL GO GET THE PAINT!

COULD YOU PUT MY CART OF GROCERIES BACK? THE HOUSE-KEEPING MAGAZINE AT THE CHECKOUT INSPIRED ME TO START AGAIN FROM SCRATCH

BIP BIP BIP BIP BOOP BEEP BIP
THIS LINE IS CURRENTLY BUSY. PHONEX WILL NOTIFY YOU WHEN IT BECOMES AVAILABLE. THE COST IS 35¢. PRESS THE STAR KEY TO ACTIVATE
GET AHOLD OF YOUR FRIEND?
NOPE, THANKS TO ADVANCES IN PHONE TECHNOLOGY I REALIZED THAT IF I DIDN'T NEED TO TALK TO HER 35¢' WORTH I DIDN'T NEED TO TALK TO HER AT ALL

SQUEAK!
THAT DRAWER IS STILL STICKING
I WANT YOU TO DO SOMETHING ABOUT IT OR I WILL
I'M CURIOUS. I'M GOING TO SPRAY ON A LITTLE SILICONE. WHAT WERE YOU GOING TO DO ABOUT IT?
COMPLETE KITCHEN RENOVATION

BELIEF
PFOOF
BELIEF
I GATHER YOU DIDN'T BUY THAT LAST COMMERCIAL WHERE THE WOMAN WASHED AND DRIED HER HAIR IN THE AIRPLANE'S WASHROOM
BELIEF

COULD YOU DO THAT?
UNDER CERTAIN CIRCUMSTANCES, MAYBE
REALLY? YOU'D DO IT?
IF I HAD TO, YES
FORGET IT! YOU DON'T HAVE THE NERVE!
I DO TOO! AND I'LL PROVE IT TO YOU AFTER OUR SON GOES TO BED
WELL, I'LL BE! YOU DID THE FULL MONKEY!
THAT'S 'MONTY'!

LAST NIGHT BETTY'S HUSBAND DID THE 'FULL MONTY' FOR HER
I'LL DO IT FOR YOU TOO
I'M READY!
HERE I COME
!
WELL?
I'VE GOT TO START WATCHING MORE THAN THE HISTORY CHANNEL
HA-HA HA HA HA HA

I COULDN'T BE WITH A MAN WHO WASN'T PERKED UP BY THE THEME TO 'THE MAGNIFICENT SEVEN'

Betty
By Delainey and Rasmussen
OKAY, LET ME PUT IT THIS WAY —
THERE'S ONLY SO MANY STAPLE MEATS — CHICKEN, BEEF, PORK, LAMB, SALMON AND OTHER FISH
A FEW OTHER MEATS LIKE TURKEY, DUCK, GOOSE, GOAT — THAT SOME PEOPLE CAN ENJOY ONCE IN A WHILE
I'LL SKIP THE SPICES, BUT IT'S THE SAME THING THERE —
THEN THERE'S THE GRAINS — FRUITS AND VEGETABLES — ALSO QUITE LIMITED
FACE IT, THERE'S ONLY SO MUCH FOOD IN THE GLOBAL VILLAGE AND ONLY SO MANY WAYS TO PREPARE IT
AND SO THAT, IN A NUTSHELL, IS WHY YOU'RE ALL FOR THE SPACE PROGRAM?
LISTEN, THE BIG QUESTION ISN'T IS THERE LIFE ON OTHER PLANETS, BUT IS THERE SOME GOOD EATING?
Delainey & Rasmussen

HEY, THIS LOOKS INTERESTING! "LADIES' POWERSKATING AND ICE HOCKEY"
"LEARN HOW TO INCREASE YOUR SKATING POWER AND BALANCE. DEVELOP THE STICK-HANDLING, SHOOTING, CHECKING AND PASSING SKILLS NECESSARY TO ENJOY THIS EXCITING SPORT!"
WHO KNOWS? I TAKE THIS AND MAYBE SOMEDAY WE COULD EVEN PLAY TOGETHER ON THE SAME TEAM!
YEAH, THEN WE CAN COME HOME AND PLAY BARBIES
BARBIES?
YOU'RE SERIOUS?
I DON'T KNOW, BETTY. I GOT DRAGGED TO SO MANY HOCKEY GAMES TO WATCH MY BROTHERS PLAY THAT I GOT SICK OF THE WHOLE THING
AND IT WASN'T JUST THE HOCKEY, IT WAS THE ENDLESS TALK ABOUT IT AROUND THE KITCHEN TABLE AFTERWARD
SO DO I WANT TO LACE UP THE SKATES AND PLAY MYSELF? I DON'T KNOW...
SURE, I UNDERSTAND. YOU WANT TO STAY HOME AND PLAY BARBIES
"BARBIES"?
YOU SURE YOU DON'T WANT TO PLAY?
I NEED SOME HOCKEY SKATES
SURE
HAVE A SEAT
THESE ARE TWO SIZES SMALLER THAN YOUR SHOE SIZE. THAT'S HOW SKATES FIT
REALLY, WOW!
YOU BOUGHT A PAIR OF SKATES PLUS A PAIR OF SKATE BOOTS?
BETTY, I'M WEARING SIZE 9! END OF STORY

WELCOME TO LADIES' POWERSKATING AND ICE HOCKEY
BEFORE WE START, HOW MANY OF YOU HAVEN'T SKATED WITH HOCKEY SKATES BEFORE — SHOW OF HANDS
EASY DOES IT AT FIRST, LADIES
GRADUALLY PICK UP SPEED
POWER THROUGH THE CORNERS
WHAM!
BY THE WAY, WHEN PLAYING HOCKEY, AVOID WEARING HAIR GEL OR STYLING MOUSSE. PERSPIRATION CAN MAKE IT RUN INTO THE EYES, CAUSING TEMPORARY BLINDNESS
FEEL LIKE A COLD ONE?
SURE, SEEMS APPROPRIATE
HERE'S TO HOCKEY!
TO HOCKEY!
YOU REALIZE, OF COURSE, THAT BY ALL THIS WE ARE ENGAGED IN A SORT OF TRANSVESTISM
EASY, BETTY, THE ONLY LINES WE'RE CROSSING ARE ON THE ICE

HEY, LOOK! THERE'S SHINNY EVERY AFTER-NOON AT 4:00 P.M. EVERYONE WELCOME
IF WE CAN SCRAPE TOGETHER FULL EQUIPMENT, WE COULD PLAY SOME INFORMAL COME-AS-YOU-ARE HOCKEY
COME ON IN, LADIES. HAVE A SEAT
A LITTLE TOO 'INFORMAL' AND 'COME-AS-YOU-ARE' FOR MY TASTE
DER.

USED SPORTS EQUIPMENT
MY DEFINITION OF "USED" JUST GOT REDEFINED DOWNWARD
MY LUNCH GOT REDEFINED UPWARD
DER.

WE NEED HOCKEY EQUIPMENT
OKAY, WHAT ALL DO YOU NEED?
EVERYTHING. HELMETS, VISORS, SHOULDER AND CHEST PADS, ELBOW PADS, GLOVES, PANTS, SHIN PADS, PRACTICE JERSEYS, SOCKS, ...AND, UM.. UM... UH
UM.. ..ER..
FEMALE PROTECTIVE CUPS?
YES
FOLLOW ME
YOU'D THINK WITH ALL THE OTHER STUFF WE'RE USED TO BUYING THAT WOULD'VE BEEN EASIER...
YEAH
DER.

READY?

READY!

WELL, WHAT DO YOU THINK?

YOU WEREN'T READY, WERE YOU?

ALEX, YOU WERE REALLY SOMETHING ON THOSE RESISTANCE SKATING DRILLS

THANKS

RESISTANCE HAS NEVER BEEN A PROBLEM FOR ME

ACCEPTANCE — NOW THAT'S TOUGH

HEY! THE OLD GORDIE HOWE 'MR HOCKEY' WRIST-STRENGTHENING EXERCISE!

I REMEMBER SPENDING HOURS AS A KID ROLLING THE BROOM HANDLE WITH MY WRISTS RAISING AND LOWERING THE FIVE-POUND WEIGHT

I'M USING A TEN-POUND WEIGHT

GOOD FOR YOU

27

WOULD YOU MIND COOKING UP SUPPER? MY LEG IS REALLY BOTHERING ME
SURE, NO PROBLEM
PUT ON MY APRON SO YOU DON'T GET SPLATTERED
OKAY
YES, RIGHT NOW WHILE I SIT WATCHING SPORTS, NURSING MY HOCKEY INJURY, HE'S IN THE KITCHEN WEARING MY FRILLY APRON COOKING ME SUPPER
WOW!

YOU SHOULD'VE COME—YOU MISSED A GOOD MOVIE
YEAH, MOM
GREETINGS, MONEYPENNY
VODKA MARTINI, SHAKEN, NOT STIRRED
HA HA HA HA HA HA HA HA HA HA
I KNOW BETTER THAN TO GET IN THE WAY OF TWO GUYS JAMES-BONDING

THANKS FOR BRINGING ME HERE
WELL, I FIGURED SOME LIGHT PUBLIC SKATING MIGHT BE GOOD FOR YOUR PULLED MUSCLE
HOW DOES IT FEEL?
ACTUALLY, PRETTY GOOD
WATCH THIS
KA-PWING!
YOW! THERE GOES ONE FAST MOTHER!

Betty
By Delainey and Rasmussen.
HERE WE ARE, SHOPPING
NOT A MEANINGLESS QUEST TO SPEND MONEY...
BUT AN EXERCISE IN PROBLEM-SOLVING
SOMETIMES WE GO WITH A PROBLEM IN MIND, AND SOMETIMES WE JUST GO AND NOTICE A SOLUTION TO A PROBLEM WE DIDN'T EVEN KNOW WE HAD
SO IS THERE ANY PROBLEM WE NEED TO SOLVE TODAY?
OUR TV IS TOO SMALL? OUR STEREO LACKS SURROUND?
OUR BACK YARD DOESN'T HAVE A SPA? OUR CAR ISN'T A CONVERTIBLE?
HA-HA—JUST KIDDING—WHAT PROBLEM REALLY NEEDS SOLVING? YOU TELL ME...
Delainey & Rasmussen

Betty
By Delainey and Rasmussen

"EATING DINNER ON THE BACK STEP?"
"YEP"

"HOW COME?"
"I LOST MY LUCKY LOTTERY NUMBERS"

"I KEPT THEM ON A CARD IN MY WALLET BUT IT MUST'VE DROPPED OUT OR SOMETHING"

"YOU DON'T REMEMBER THEM?"
"AFRAID NOT. THAT'S WHY I WROTE THEM DOWN"

"SO? GET SOME NEW NUMBERS"
"CAN'T. THEY WERE IMPORTANT DATES—BETTY'S BIRTHDAY, OUR ANNIVERSARY, THE DAY WE GOT ENGAGED..."

"SO WHY NOT ASK BETTY? SHE KNOWS ALL THAT STUFF"
"I DID"

"OH!"
"IF YOU'RE GOING IN FOR A VISIT, COULD YOU BRING OUT THE KETCHUP?"

PRO WRESTLING?
YOU HAVE SOMETHING AGAINST THE EXPLORATION OF CLASSIC THEMES SET AGAINST A MYTHIC BACKDROP WITH LARGER-THAN-LIFE CHARACTERS?
SORRY, I DIDN'T KNOW YOU GUYS LIKE THAT KIND OF STUFF
WE LOVE IT!
HELLO - OPERA GUILD? YES - FOUR TICKETS FOR YOUR NEXT PERFORMANCE
Delainey & Rasmussen

OH, COME ON — YOU'RE NOT REALLY GOING TO DRAG ME, OUR SON AND MY BROTHER TO THE OPERA
WHY NOT? YOU SAID YOURSELF YOU LIKED "THE EXPLORATION OF CLASSIC THEMES SET AGAINST A MYTHIC BACKDROP, ETC...."
I WAS TALKING ABOUT PRO WRESTLING!
YOU SHOULD TAKE A LOOK AT THIS
"THE BIG BOOK OF OPERA STORIES"?
THE OPERA WE'RE GOING TO IS IN ITALIAN — YOU NEED TO READ ABOUT IT OR YOU WON'T UNDERSTAND IT
OH, PERFECT! OPERA AND HOMEWORK!

LOOK, I DON'T MIND GOING TO THE OPERA WITH YOU IF YOU'LL JUST ADMIT THE REAL REASON WE'RE HERE
REAL REASON?
SO THAT YOU WOMEN GET TO SHOW OFF YOUR SOPHISTICATION, YOUR DEEP APPRECIATION OF CULTURE AND MOSTLY YOUR DOMINANCE OVER MEN
DOMINANCE OVER MEN?
SURE, THAT NOT ONLY CAN YOU DRAG MEN TO THE OPERA BUT ALSO FORCE THEM TO PARADE AROUND IN MONKEY SUITS
I MEAN SOME POOR SAPS ARE EVEN WEARING TUXEDOS, FOR CRYING OUT LOUD
WHEN YOU'RE FINISHED, I WANT YOU TO PIN ON THIS RIBBON OF SUPPORT FOR THE WOMEN'S SHELTER

MOM? WHY ARE SOME PEOPLE WEARING BINOCULARS?
THEY'RE OPERA GLASSES. THEY HELP THEM ENJOY THE PERFORMANCE
DEX, MAYBE WE SHOULD GET OUR-SELVES SOME OPERA GLASSES
GOOD IDEA

I WAS MAKING SOME PROGRESS ON THE CULTURAL FRONT— MY HUSBAND ACTUALLY ORDERED SOMETHING OTHER THAN STEAK RECENTLY—
SO WHEN I SAW MY OPENING, I TOOK IT AND GOT NOT ONLY MY HUSBAND, BUT OUR SON AND MY HUSBAND'S BROTHER TO GO TO THE OPERA WITH ME
WHAT HAPPENED?
I GAMBLED IT ALL AND LOST— THEY STAYED AWAKE FOR THE WHOLE THING AND I FELL ASLEEP
OUCH!
AND WHAT'S WORSE, THEY ENJOYED IT— MY HUSBAND WANTS TO SUBSCRIBE FOR THE REST OF THE SEASON
WOW! HUBRIS, A FALL FROM GRACE, AND AN IRONIC REVERSAL OF FORTUNE— YOU SHOULDN'T BE GOING TO OPERAS, YOU SHOULD BE WRITING THEM

Betty
By Delainey & Rasmussen
WHAT'S THE DEAL WITH THAT?
THAT?
THAT'S A CAR-BRA
LOOKS KIND OF KINKY TO ME
HUH?
C'MON, BLACK LEATHER?
FOR CRYING OUT LOUD. WHAT ELSE SHOULD IT BE?
LISTEN, HERE'S WHAT'S REALLY GOING ON. YOU MEN KNOW YOUR WIVES WON'T WEAR THAT STUFF SO YOU BUY IT FOR YOUR CARS
GET OUT OF HERE!
C'MON, YOU CAN'T DENY THAT YOU MEN THINK OF YOUR CARS AS FEMALES. "SHE'S A BEAUTY" YOU'LL SAY, OR "CHECK OUT WHAT SHE'S GOT UNDER HER HOOD."
SO NOW YOU'RE TAKING IT ONE STEP FURTHER AND BUYING YOUR CARS LINGERIE
HA-HA VERY FUNNY
OKAY, I CAN'T SPEAK FOR ALL MEN — BUT MOST MEN JUST USE THEM TO PROTECT THE FRONT OF THEIR CARS FROM ROCKS
D&R

A CIGAR?
YEP
THEY'RE ALL THE RAGE—HERE, I GOT YOU ONE
ME?
NOW IT'S OKAY FOR WOMEN TO SMOKE CIGARS–
...OKAY BUT HARDLY DEMURE

GO AHEAD, TAKE A FEW PUFFS
JUST A SEC
BIP BIP BIP BIP BIP BIP BIP
HELLO?
CALL YOUR MOM?
BEFORE I DO THIS, I NEED TO KNOW SHE'S NOT AT LARGE
WHO'S THERE?
CLICK

IT'S BEEN SAID "ONLY SUCCESSFUL PEOPLE SMOKE CIGARS"
SUCCESSFUL PEOPLE SMOKE "EL COMPOSTO"?
THEY DO IF THEY BUY 'EM DOWN AT THE HAPPY HAMPER

FUNNY THING ABOUT SMOKING A CIGAR — WHEN YOU START YOU LOOK LIKE A BIG SHOT, BUT SMOKE IT TOO LONG, AND YOU END UP LOOKING LIKE A BUM

I'D LIKE TO THINK I SMOKED THAT CIGAR TO "ENJOY A CIVILIZED EXPERIENCE OF REFINED AND PLEASURABLE TASTE"
BUT IN TRUTH, I THINK IT'S BECAUSE I SAW DEMI MOORE SMOKING ONE ON THE COVER OF "CIGAR AFICIONADO" MAGAZINE
DO WE EVER GET PAST OUR DESIRE TO JOIN THE "COOL" PEOPLE?
YOU'RE ASKING ME? LOOK AT MY RUNNING SHOES...

WHEN WE SMOKED THOSE CIGARS, WE SENT THE MESSAGE TO OUR SON THAT SMOKING IS ACCEPTABLE
YEAH
WE FORGOT FOR A MOMENT THAT OUR RIGHTS AS INDIVIDUALS ARE NEGATED BY OUR RESPONSIBILITIES AS PARENTS
YEAH
GOSH, BUT IT WAS FUN WHILE IT LASTED
YEAH, LIKE REMEMBER THE TIME WE BOUGHT THE SUGAR FROSTED FLAKES?...

CLICK
THIS IS FOOLISH. WE CAN'T WATCH HIM FOREVER
HE'S GOING TO MAKE SOME UNPLEASANT DISCOVERIES AND WE JUST HAVE TO HOPE HE HAS THE SOPHISTICATION TO DEAL WITH THEM
!
!!
CLICK
ALL RIGHT, YOUNG MAN, YOUR MOTHER AND I WISH TO KNOW JUST WHERE YOU ACQUIRED THE SOPHISTICATION TO DEAL WITH THAT!

surfing the net
CLICK
WHAT IS THIS? A "BIG BROTHER WATCHING" KIND OF DEAL?
A "BIG MOM" AND "BIG DAD" WATCHING KIND OF DEAL

WHAT'RE YOU LISTENING TO?
WRNR BALTIMORE OVER THE INTERNET
OUR RIDICULOUSLY EXPENSIVE COMPUTER HAS BECOME A TRANSISTOR RADIO

COOL, HUH?
CAN YOU BELIEVE IT! RIGHT NOW I'M LISTENING TO A RADIO BROADCAST FROM TURKEY
IT SOUNDS LIKE ECHOES, STUTTERS AND NOISE
I KNOW! IT COULD BE THE FEED OR IT COULD BE WHAT THEY LISTEN TO —I HAVE NO WAY OF KNOWING!
GIVE HIM TIME. WHEN MY DAD GOT ME A MULTIBAND RADIO I LISTENED TO A TAXI DISPATCHER FOR THREE DAYS STRAIGHT

MOM, I NEED YOUR CREDIT CARD NUMBER
I WANT TO BUY A CD I HEARD ON INTERNET RADIO, BUT THE ONLY WAY I CAN GET IT IS FROM AN INTERNET RETAILER
SHOW ME
SEE, THEY HAVE IT AND IT'S A SAVINGS OF $1.79
OKAY, LET'S GIVE IT A TRY
THE STRANGE FEELING WHEN WE FIRST USED A CREDIT CARD? WELL, IT'S BACK

URL
BIT BYTE
HTML
ETHERNET
DOMAIN NAME
BANDWIDTH
ATM HTTP
T3
FAST INTERNET CONNECTION
ARE YOU A PROCRASTINATOR?
EVER FEEL A TRAIN WAS LEAVING THE STATION THAT YOU SHOULD'VE BEEN ON BUT YOU WEREN'T?
BETTY, MY TRAINS HAVE BEEN LEAVING THE STATION LIKE CLOCKWORK SINCE I WAS 16

BUMP
FOLLOW ME TO BOB'S WORLD OF TECHNOLOGY
I JUST GOT RUN OVER BY A WORLD OF TECHNOLOGY —WHERE'RE YOUR COMPUTER BOOKS?
YOU WOULD LIKE HELP SELECTING BOOKS ON HOW COMPUTERS WORK?
YES
OKAY, LET ME GET TED
HI, MY NAME IS T-E-D. MY JOB IS TO HELP PEOPLE SELECT BOOKS ABOUT C-O-M-P-U-T-E-R-S
TED, JUST BECAUSE I DON'T KNOW MUCH ABOUT COMPUTERS DOESN'T MEAN I'M AN IDIOT OR A DUMMY
THINK SO? YOU HAVEN'T BEEN IN A COMPUTER BOOKS SECTION BEFORE, HAVE YOU?
24 HOURS TO HTML COMPETENCY
BOOKS
BOOKS
SIGH
24 HOURS TO FREEING UP 24 HOURS

HTML CODE
<HTML><HEAD><TITLE> BETTY</TITLE></HEAD> <BODY> ZZZZZZZZ ZZZZZZZZ</BODY> </HTML>

COMPUTER CODE 101
INTRODUCTION TO JAVA APPLETS

I'M GETTING THE HANG OF THE WORLD OF COMPUTERS, IMHO.
IMHO?
IN MY HUMBLE OPINION
IMHO PEOPLE WITH AN 'O' ARE RARELY 'H'!
Delainey & Rasmussen

SO WHERE'S YOUR COMPUTER READING AT?
C++
"C++" WOW! THAT BRINGS BACK MEMORIES
IN SCHOOL I READ AT A C++ LEVEL TOO
C++ IS A PROGRAMMING LANGUAGE, NOT A GRADE
I'D UNDERSTAND THE WORDS, BUT I'D HAVE TO READ THEM AGAIN TO UNDERSTAND THEIR MEANING
C++ IS A PROGRAMMING LANGUAGE, NOT A GRADE
DER

"...FOLLOWED BY THE POUND KEY"
MOM, HOW COME THE "#" SYMBOL ON THE PHONE IS CALLED THE "POUND" KEY?
I DON'T KNOW
IS IT A COMPUTER TERM?
COULD BE
OF COURSE FOR SOME PEOPLE THEY'RE ALL POUND KEYS
BAM BAM BAM
DER

SEND
CLICK
BETTY, CHECK YOUR E-MAIL!
BEEP: YOU HAVE MAIL
ALEX, IT JUST GOT HERE!!
DER

BRAIN TEST
Press any key to continue

CLICK

Interesting. You chose the "enter" key. Press any key to continue.

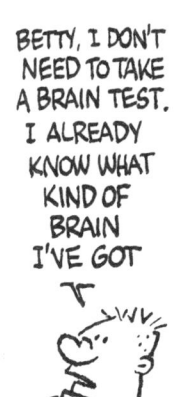

"Alex e-mailed me this great brain testing program — why don't you come and take it? I DID!"

"Betty, I don't need to take a brain test. I already know what kind of brain I've got"

"Oh, really? So what is it? Right or left dominant? Auditory or visual?"

UM

"It's the kind of brain that can tell right away that me taking that test is definitely not in my best interest. What kind is that?"

"See! It's only twenty questions. There are no right or wrong answers"

"And when you finish, it will tell you what kind of brain you have and give you a short evaluation"

"Nothing to worry about, just helpful, harmless, non-judgmental fun!"

"You must've got a good one"

"Oh, yeah!"

41

Betty

By Delainey and Rasmussen

Panel 2: "HEY, LOOK! A GARBAGE GNOME!" "CUTE IDEA"

Panel 3: "LET'S GET ONE FOR OURSELVES" "YEAH"

Panel 4: LATER — "IT SEEMS THE GARBAGE COLLECTOR DIDN'T TAKE OUR ELF"

43

SNIFF
ADMIT IT, TITANIC WAS JUST AS GOOD THE SECOND TIME AS THE FIRST! THE TIME JUST FLEW BY, DIDN'T IT?
FORMER WORLD SNOOKER CHAMPION RAY REARDON WAS TRAPPED IN A COAL MINE. WHILE HE WAITED FOR HELP TO ARRIVE, HE PLAYED SNOOKER MATCHES IN HIS HEAD
YOU WATCHED 'TITANIC'. I PLAYED SNOOKER

!?

— HONEY
SIGH
HAVE YOU SEEN MY OTHER BOXERS? THESE HAVE FINALLY GIVEN UP THE GHOST
AND THEY SAY PEOPLE WHO READ ARE MORE TOLERANT

Betty

By Delainey and Rasmussen

AND THE LESSON IS?...

UH, THERE ARE SOME RESTAURANTS WHERE YOU DON'T ASK FOR A "DOGGIE BAG"?

Betty
By Delainey & Rasmussen
HERE COMES SOMEBODY NOW
EXCUSE ME, BUT WE CAN'T AGREE ON A PLACE TO EAT
I WANT CHINESE, MY HUSBAND WANTS ITALIAN, MY FRIEND WANTS MEXICAN AND HER HUSBAND WANTS A STEAK
SO WHAT WE THOUGHT WAS — WE'D ASK THE FIRST PERSON WHO COMES ALONG — WHICH IS YOU
SO, DO YOU HAVE A SUGGESTION FOR US?
YOU HAVE TO ADMIT, THIS KIND OF PUTS ARGUING ABOUT RESTAURANTS IN PERSPECTIVE

FOR VALENTINE'S DAY JOHN GOT ME A DOZEN ROSES, SOME BELGIAN CHOCOLATES AND A REALLY NICE HANDMADE CARD
MY HUSBAND GOT ME A 'DILBERT' VALENTINE
OH, I'M SORRY
WHY BE SORRY? IT'S GOING TO GIVE ME ALL THE LEVERAGE I NEED TO GET HIM TO TAKE BALLROOM DANCING LESSONS WITH ME
YOU DON'T WANT TO DO ANYTHING WITH ME, IS THAT IT?

GUESS WHAT! I DID IT! I SIGNED US UP FOR THE PUBLIC SCHOOL'S BALLROOM DANCING COURSE!
SEE! WE'LL LEARN TO FOX TROT, WALTZ, JIVE AND TWO-STEP!
SOUNDS LIKE FUN, DON'T YOU THINK?
I SUPPOSE
BUT ISN'T IT A TAD OMINOUS THAT AMONG THE SUGGESTED PREP COURSES ARE SURVIVING MARITAL STRESS I & II, AND CONTROLLING ANGER I, II & III?

LET'S GO! IT'S TIME FOR OUR FIRST DANCE CLASS!
I KNOW I KNOW
DON'T BE SO GLUM- THIS COULD BE FUN, YOU KNOW
RIGHT
DID YOU REMEMBER YOUR DANCING SHOES?
YES,YES... I BOUGHT A PAIR ON MY LUNCH BREAK
BOUGHT?
SEE?... AIR ASTAIRE

48

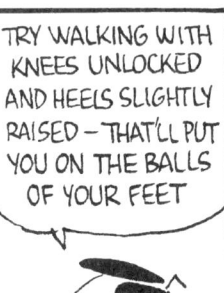

UP AN' AT 'EM, BIG BOY. OUR DANCE CLASS IS TOMORROW AND WE NEED PRACTICE
OKAY, TOOTS– HERE GOES... LET'S CUT A RUG
BRRRIP!
WELL, I'LL BE!... I REALLY DID CUT A RUG
TIME TO TRIM THOSE TOENAILS

YOU KNOW, ONE THING I DON'T UNDER-STAND ABOUT DANCING IS WHY IT'S SOMETIMES CALLED "TRIPPING THE LIGHT FANTASTIC"
WHOOPS
OKAY, I GET THE "TRIPPING THE LIGHT" PART

PARDON MY FOOT
EXCUSE ME...
YOU'RE STANDING TOO FAR APART. TRY STANDING CLOSER TOGETHER. YOU'LL BE MUCH BETTER OFF– IT'S A CONTROL THING
PARDON MY KNEE
YES, MUCH BETTER. THANKS

50

WHATCHA READING?
IT'S A BOOK ON FENG SHUI, THE CHINESE PHILOSOPHY OF ORDER AND HARMONY
A HOUSE WITH GOOD FENG SHUI MAKES THE PEOPLE WHO LIVE IN IT LUCKY, HAPPY AND PROSPEROUS
DOES OUR HOUSE HAVE GOOD FENG SHUI
YEAH, RIGHT

THE "WOMEN'S GARDEN OF INSIGHTFUL THOUGHTS"?
YEP
HOW COME THERE'S A "WOMEN'S GARDEN OF INSIGHTFUL THOUGHTS," BUT NO "MEN'S GARDEN OF INSIGHTFUL THOUGHTS"?
OKAY, MAYBE WHAT I SAID WAS FUNNY, BUT IT'S NOT FALL-OUT-OF-BED FUNNY!

BETTY, YOU JUST GO RIGHT AHEAD READING "THE WOMAN'S GARDEN OF INSIGHTFUL THOUGHTS." I'VE BOUGHT A BOOK OF MY OWN
IT'S NOT "THE MAN'S GARDEN OF INSIGHTFUL THOUGHTS," BUT IT'S PROBABLY AS CLOSE AS ONE CAN GET
"THE WOMAN'S GARDEN OF INSIGHTFUL THOUGHTS —MEN'S EDITION"?!!
EVERY DAY A NEW INSIGHT INTO WHAT YOU'RE THINKING AND WHAT I CAN DO ABOUT IT

WHATCHA WRITING?
IF YOU MUST KNOW, IT'S A GRATITUDE JOURNAL– I HAVE TO WRITE DOWN FIVE THINGS I'M GRATEFUL FOR EACH DAY
REALLY? A 'GRATITUDE JOURNAL'? YOU'RE KIDDING, RIGHT? THAT'S THE–
YOU'RE CROSSING SOMETHING OUT– WHAT ARE YOU CROSSING OUT?

WHAT DO YOU THINK YOU'RE DOING?
WRITING IN A GRATITUDE JOURNAL, SAME AS YOU
IF IT MAKES SENSE FOR YOU TO KEEP ONE, IT OUGHT TO MAKE SENSE FOR ME TO KEEP ONE TOO
ARE YOU SERIOUS?
SURE
THERE, DONE
THAT WAS FIVE THINGS ALREADY?
SURE, THREE MEALS, TWO SNACKS. END OF STORY, TIME FOR BED, WHY?

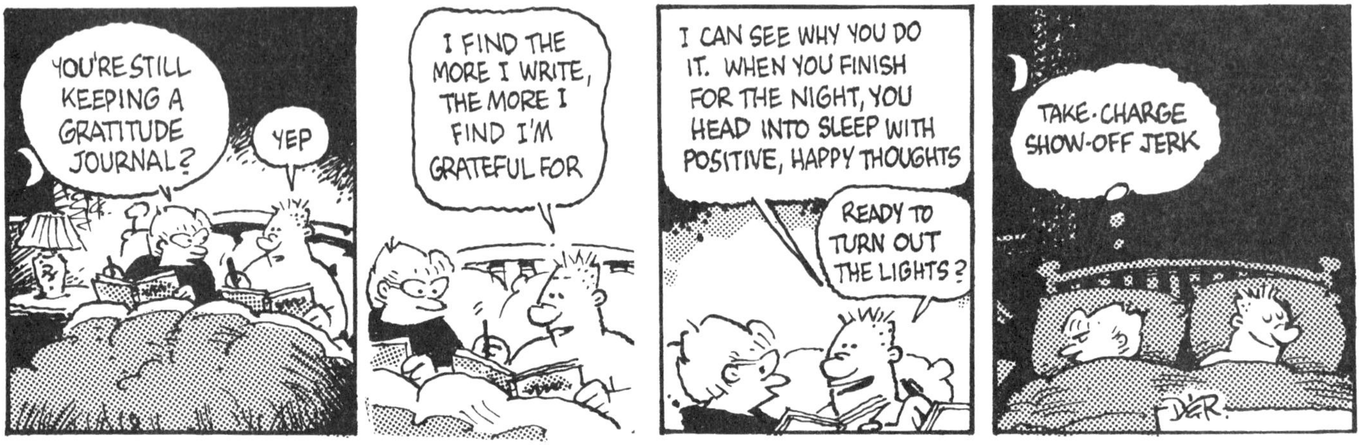
YOU'RE STILL KEEPING A GRATITUDE JOURNAL?
YEP
I FIND THE MORE I WRITE, THE MORE I FIND I'M GRATEFUL FOR
I CAN SEE WHY YOU DO IT. WHEN YOU FINISH FOR THE NIGHT, YOU HEAD INTO SLEEP WITH POSITIVE, HAPPY THOUGHTS
READY TO TURN OUT THE LIGHTS?
TAKE-CHARGE SHOW-OFF JERK

HEY, IS THAT THE "WOMEN'S GARDEN OF INSIGHTFUL THOUGHTS"?
YEAH, IT'S PRETTY GOOD
I'LL SAY
I USUALLY READ IT IN BED, JUST BEFORE I TURN OUT THE LIGHT TO GO TO SLEEP
DOES IT HELP YOU GET TO SLEEP?
I'LL SAY! NOTHING SPOILS THE MOOD LIKE THE WOMEN'S GARDEN OF INSIGHTFUL THOUGHTS

WANT TO KNOW SOMETHING STRANGE?
LATELY ALL MY PANTS SEEM TO BE WEARING OUT ON THE FRONT OF MY UPPER THIGHS
INTERESTING. SIT DOWN, LUNCH IS READY
EEEEAH!
ANY THEORIES?
LET ME GUESS, YOUR VOICE IS KIND OF HOARSE TOO?

I'D BE HA'PY TO HELP Y' BUT— SORRY, MY P'ONE'S BLEEPING. I HAVE AN'THER CALL. 'BYE
LIFE'S SO MUCH EASIER SINCE I LEARNED TO FAKE CALL WAITING
MAKING YOUR LIFE EASIER BY FAKING THINGS. I'M NOT SURE I LIKE THE SOUND OF THAT

Betty
By Delainey & Rasmussen
ALEX WANTS TO KILL AN AFTERNOON AT THE ART GALLERY AND I'M GOING TO JOIN HER
THAT GOES WAY BEYOND JUST KILLING AN AFTERNOON– IT BORDERS ON MURDER
GALLERY GIFT SHOP AND CAFE
Delainey & Rasmussen

LET'S GO IN HERE!
The BRICK SHEET HOUSE
IT'S TIME WE SPRUCED UP OUR BEDROOM, DO YOU AGREE?
SURE, I GUESS
SO, WHAT DO YOU THINK OF THIS?
UH...STRIPES MAKE THE BED LOOK FAT?

NO...
I DON'T THINK SO
I CAN'T HELP IT. FLOWER-PRINT SHEETS MAKE A BED SEEM TOO MUCH LIKE MY AUNT SADIE'S LAP

NOW THIS IS WHAT WE NEED ON OUR BED...LACE, RUFFLES AND A BED SKIRT!
LACE? RUFFLES? BED SKIRTS?
MAN, YOU WOMEN NEVER QUITE GET OVER THE TIME YOU SPENT PLAYING WITH DOLLS, DO YOU?

56

57

Betty
By Delainey and Rasmussen
WHAT'S THAT?
A HEDGE
AND WHAT'S THAT?
A MATURE OAK TREE
WON'T THOSE THINGS TAKE A LONG TIME?
YES, THEY WILL
LANDSCAPING IS ABOUT PATIENCE
RIGHT!
LISTEN, JUST BECAUSE I'M PLANNING SOME LANDSCAPING, DON'T THINK I'M HAPPY IN THIS DUMP

I'VE RUN YOU A BATH
OKAY
SAY, THIS IS A TREAT!
I DON'T REMEMBER THE LAST TIME YOU RAN ME A BATH...
YOU KNOW, IF YOU DON'T LIKE THE BATH OIL I BOUGHT YOU FOR CHRISTMAS, YOU COULD JUST TELL ME
I LIG ID FIDE. GED ID, EDJOY
Delainey & Rasmussen

DAD, CAN WE GIVE THIS ONE A LISTEN?
THE GRATEFUL DEAD-SURE!
I JUST CAN'T TURN IT UP LOUD ON ACCOUNT OF THE NEIGHBORS
BANG!
BANG!
BANG!
DARN, TOO LOUD
DER

THAT'S "TEN YEARS AFTER" FRONTED BY OL' FREAKY FINGERS HIMSELF, ALVIN LEE
HIS FINGERS WOULD JUST FLY UP AND DOWN THE FRETS
LIKE THAT?
UM
...ER, NO
I'VE LOST THE ABILITY TO PLAY LEAD AIR GUITAR

HEY! CHECK IT OUT!
A RED SOLID BODY ELECTRIC GUITAR
WITH AMP
SHORTY SOLD IT TO ME BECAUSE HE'S GETTING MARRIED. HE GAVE ME A DEAL!
PLINK
IT'S 20 YEARS BEHIND SCHEDULE, BUT THE DREAM IS BACK ON TRACK!
WOW! WAIT'LL I TELL MY GIRLFRIENDS— MY BOYFRIEND'S A ROCK 'N' ROLLER!
NOT ONLY IS THIS THE HOTTEST-LOOKING GUITAR—BUT THIS IS A TUBE AMPLIFIER!
BBBWWUEEEEEE
BW-WU-U
PLINK
PLINK
PLINK
PLINK
PLINK
THANK HEAVEN FOR TUBE AMPS
!
BREE-I-ING!
BWEEE!
WUUUUUU!
THAT'S RIGHT, SON, YOUR OLD MAN HAS AN AXE!
AN AXE? SOUNDS MORE LIKE A CHAIN SAW

CAN I TRY?
SURE, SON, I DON'T SEE WHY NOT
THE 'ACTION' IS KIND OF SLOW, ONE OF THE PICK-UPS NEEDS REPLACING, AND THERE'S A SLIGHT WARP IN THE NECK
THAT'S OKAY, AT MY FIRST STADIUM CONCERT I PLAN TO LIGHT IT ON FIRE
WHY WAIT?
HERE GOES...THE JIMMY PAGE GUITAR PART FROM "STAIRWAY TO HEAVEN"
THERE WALKS A LADY WE ALL KNOW...
PLINK
WOO-EE!
DUNK
Bleep!
WELL?
NO OFFENSE, BUT GUITAR KARAOKE IS EVEN MORE ANNOYING THAN THE SINGING KIND
BROING!
RISE 'N' SHINE

Betty
By Delainey and Rasmussen
BIP
BIP
BIP
YES, HELLO. I'D LIKE TEN TICKETS, PLEASE...
ON MY CREDIT CARD... THE NUMBER IS...
HI! SIX TICKETS, PLEASE
NINE, PLEASE
ALL THAT'S LEFT ARE SEATS WITH OBSTRUCTED VIEWS
TICKETS
SPONSORED BY CELL-X CELLULAR PHONES
Delainey & Rasmussen

GUITAR FUN
DER
SCREEECH!
I DECIDED TO TAKE A BREAK FROM SIGHT-READING AND WORK ON FEEDBACK

REMEMBER HOW I USED TO PLAY LULLABIES FOR JUNIOR WHEN HE WAS LITTLE?
YEAH, THAT WAS SWEET
IT'S TOO BAD WE DIDN'T HAVE A VIDEO CAMERA IN THOSE DAYS. IT WOULD'VE BEEN NICE TO HAVE SOME VIDEO OF THAT
WELL, WE HAVE ONE NOW...
?
BUT, DAD, I'M NOT A LITTLE KID ANYMORE...
THAT'S OKAY, I'M GOING FOR 'EMOTIONAL' TRUTH
WWRRRR
DER

WATCH THIS... I'LL DO MY BEST ROCK STAR POSE
PATHETIC, HUH?
YEP
AT LEAST WHEN I PLAY HOCKEY, I LOOK LIKE A HOCKEY PLAYER
SINCE WHEN?
DER

Panel 1: (man playing electric guitar)

Panel 2: (man walking with guitar)

Panel 3: (man playing saxophone)

Panel 4:
- "I'M AFRAID I LOOK MORE COUNTRY THAN ROCK 'N' ROLL"
- "WHICH COUNTRY?"

Panel 5: "YOU KNOW, THERE'S ALL KINDS OF PEOPLE WHO ARE ROCK GUITARISTS"

Panel 6: "MY POINT IS, THEY'RE NOT ALL EDDIE VAN HALENS OR ERIC CLAPTONS"

Panel 7: "THERE'S ALSO JERRY GARCIAS AND RANDY BACHMANS" — "HMMPF"

Panel 8: "OR ARE YOU, AT YOUR AGE, STILL HUNG UP ON THE ROCK GUITARIST-AS-A-BABE-MAGNET THING?" — "YES, BUT ONLY AS 'CATCH AND RELEASE'"

Panel 9:
- "MY HUSBAND BOUGHT HIMSELF AN ELECTRIC GUITAR AND WANTS TO PLAY IN A ROCK BAND"
- "REALLY!"
- "WOW!"

Panel 10:
- "IT'S ONE OF THOSE MIDLIFE CRISIS-START-SOMETHING-NEW-GUY THINGS, YOU KNOW HOW IT IS"
- "SURE"

Panel 11:
- "SIGH"
- "ALEX, LOOK AT THE POSTMARK ON THIS PUPPY!"

Betty
By Delainey and Rasmussen.
IS IT TOO MUCH?
NOPE
NOT ENOUGH?
NOPE
I CARRY IT OFF?
SURE
YOU SURE IT "WORKS" FOR ME?
OF COURSE, YOU'RE AN ACTIVE WOMAN?
REALLY?
YES
REALLY?
YES
SO CAN WE GO TO THE HOT TUB PARTY NOW?
OKAY, NOW REMEMBER, THE STORY IS I WIPED OUT ON MY MOUNTAIN BIKE AND WOULD LOVE TO HAVE A SOAK BUT I CAN'T WET THE DRESSING SO THERE WAS NO POINT IN BRINGING MY BATHING SUIT, GOT IT?
Delainey & Rasmussen

Betty
By Delainey and Rasmussen
?
PHOTOS
MOM, WHY IS DAD WEARING A NECK BRACE IN THIS PICTURE?
OH, THAT?... BECAUSE YOUR FATHER WAS TELLING ME ABOUT THIS BAND HE USED TO LIKE...
AND HE GAVE HIMSELF WHIPLASH SHOWING ME HOW THE GUITAR PLAYERS USED TO FLIP THEIR HEADS TO THE MUSIC
REALLY?
YEP. IF YOU DON'T BELIEVE ME, GO ASK HIM YOURSELF
DAD? CAN YOU EXPLAIN SOMETHING?
SURE, SON, WHAT?

DAD?
YES, SON?
DO YOU THINK THE EARTH COULD REALLY BE HIT BY A HUGE COMET OR ASTEROID DESTROYING ALL LIFE ON THE PLANET?
COULD IT?
IT COULD COULDN'T IT?
"DON'T WORRY, SUPERMAN WILL SAVE US"?
HE TOOK ME BY SURPRISE

HA! LOOK, A CASSETTE LYING BY THE SIDE OF THE ROAD!
I'M ALWAYS CURIOUS TO SEE WHAT MUSIC SOMEBODY HAS DISCARDED LIKE YESTERDAY'S NEWS!
THE WHO?!
QUIT SMIRKING! THERE COULD BE LOTS OF REASONS WHY IT GOT CHUCKED!
DID I SAY ANYTHING?

I'M GOING OUT TO THE BACKYARD FOR A NAP
SO DON'T OPEN THE BACK DOOR
Delainey & Rasmussen.

PUFF PUFF
WRRR
HOW WAS RIDING THE BIKE?
PRETTY GOOD, BUT BORING
IF THEY COULD FIGURE A WAY TO GIVE YOU A NEW EXPERIENCE EACH TIME YOU RODE, IT THEN THEY'D REALLY HAVE SOMETHING
THEY HAVE
I MEANT A LINK TO SOME KIND OF VIDEO GAME —BUT THIS IS GOOD, TOO
SALE
I'M INTERESTED IN SOME OFF-ROAD BIKES
OFF-ROAD BIKES, SURE, WE SELL THOSE
WE ALSO HAVE MOUNTAIN BIKES—
THIS IS A MOUNTAIN BIKE
THAT IS AN OFF-ROAD BIKE
WELL, FAMILY, SHALL WE?
JUST ONE QUESTION —WHEN WAS THE LAST TIME YOU RODE A BIKE?
DOESN'T MATTER—RIDING A BICYCLE IS LIKE RIDING A BICYCLE. ONCE YOU KNOW HOW, YOU—
CRASH!
DID YOU EVER KNOW HOW?
GOOD QUESTION

JUST A LITTLE FURTHER: WE'RE ALMOST THERE...
BAM
BASH
BOINK
BUMP!
MADE IT!
IT'LL GO EASIER NOW THAT WE'RE OFF THE CITY STREETS

ARE THESE MOUNTAIN OR DIS-MOUNTIN' BIKES?

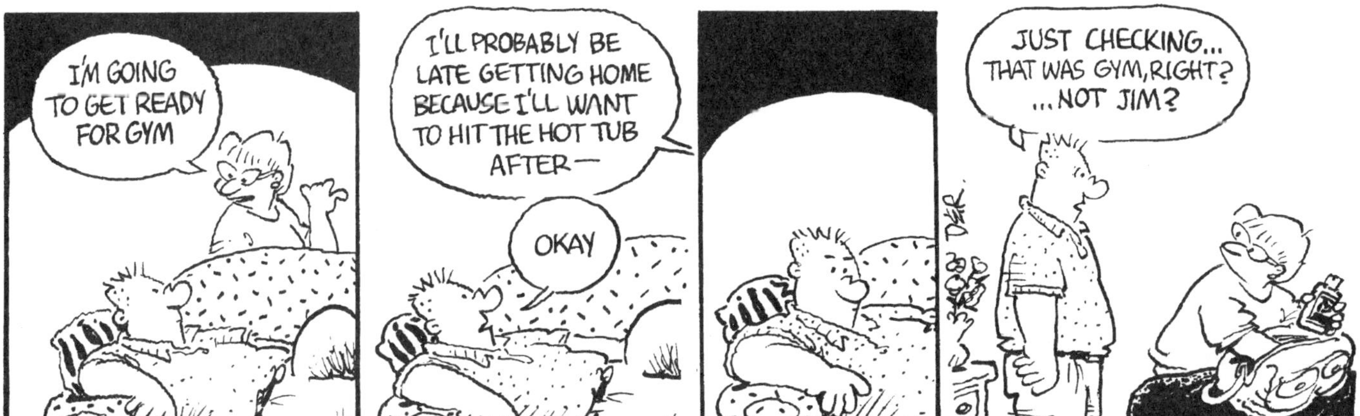
I'M GOING TO GET READY FOR GYM
I'LL PROBABLY BE LATE GETTING HOME BECAUSE I'LL WANT TO HIT THE HOT TUB AFTER—
OKAY
JUST CHECKING... THAT WAS GYM, RIGHT? ...NOT JIM?

70

71

SEE IT?
I THINK SO
I KNOW, IT'S ALMOST VISIBLE —THE SERENITY THAT COMES WITH FASTING
OH
"OH"?
I THOUGHT YOU WERE GOING TO SAY THE "STINK" THAT COMES WITH FASTING
BY ANY CHANCE IS THIS RESTAURANT NEAR A DUMPSTER FULL OF SWEAT SOCKS AND CABBAGE?

MAYBE I'M GETTING A LITTLE AHEAD OF MYSELF, BUT I CAN FORESEE THE POSSIBILITY OF ME BECOMING THE FIRST TV INFOMERCIAL-ADVOCATE OF FASTING!
I'LL HAVE MY OWN LINE OF BOOKS, TAPES AND VIDEOS! THERE'LL BE SPEAKING ENGAGEMENTS! BETTY, I'LL BE HEALTHY, THIN AND RICH!
OOH, MOMMA! SMELL THAT PIZZA!
BELIEVE ME, BETTY, IT WAS WITHIN MY GRASP
TOO BAD FOR EVERY TITANIC THERE'S AN ICEBERG

HEY! LOOK WHAT I FOUND IN THE BACK OF THE CLOSET — MY OLD HALLOWEEN CANNIBAL COSTUME!
DING! DONG!
WHO COULD THAT BE?

73

Betty
By Delainey and Rasmussen
!
I THINK YOU'VE HAD ENOUGH SUN
I THINK YOU'RE RIGHT

POOR ALEX
OH?
SHE AND JOHN CAN'T SEEM TO HAVE A BABY TOGETHER
THEY'VE BEEN TO SPECIALISTS AND EVERYTHING
IT'S SO SAD. ALL SHE CAN THINK TO DO IS TAKE UP GOLF, SO THAT'S WHAT SHE'S DONE
WHAT KIND OF CLUBS DID SHE GET?
"WHAT KIND OF CLUBS DID SHE GET?"
HEY, IT HAS A BEARING ON HOW MUCH SYMPATHY I CAN FEEL, OKAY?

I'M OFF TO GOLF WITH ALEX
HEY, I'LL COME, TOO —JUST A SEC
SORRY, THIS IS AS MUCH ABOUT THERAPY FOR ALEX AS IT IS ABOUT GOLF
I FEEL I HAVE TO BE THERE FOR HER
WHERE'S 'THERE'?
YOU DON'T WANT TO KNOW
IT'S FOXBUSH CREEK, ISN'T IT?!
WHAT IF IT IS? HEALING CAN TAKE PLACE ON PRIVATE, INTERNATIONALLY-RANKED, CHAMPIONSHIP-CALIBER GOLF COURSES, TOO...

I'VE ALWAYS PICTURED MYSELF AS A MOTHER. BUT IF THAT IS NOT TO BE, IT'S NOT TO BE
SO FROM NOW ON, IT'S GOLF
THWACK!
WOW
YOU'RE GETTING ENOUGH DISTANCE
BETTY, IT'LL BE YEARS BEFORE I GET ENOUGH DISTANCE

ALEX... ARE YOU SURE YOU DON'T WANT A PULL CART?
I'M FINE
I WANT TO SUFFER A BIT – IT'S GOOD FOR THE SOUL
OH, SURE
YE-OUCH!
IT'S ALSO PRETTY GOOD SEEING SOMEONE ELSE SUFFER, TOO. IT'S AN ALL-ROUND WIN-WIN
OOOH

I'M HOME
HOW WAS 'FOXBUSH CREEK'?
IT WAS AMAZING. IT WAS THE MOST BEAUTIFUL, MOST CHALLENGING COURSE I'VE EVER PLAYED ON
IS THERE SOME HAND SIGNAL OR GESTURE I CAN USE WHEN I ASK YOU A QUESTION TO LET YOU KNOW I'M BEING IRONIC AND DO NOT WANT AN ANSWER, PARTICULARLY AN UPBEAT ONE?

WHAT'LL YOU HAVE?
YES, UM, I'D LIKE ...UM WELL
I SEE PEOPLE TRYING BLENDS ALL THE TIME, DO YOU DO BLENDS?
SURE, WE DO BLENDS
HOW ABOUT... I DON'T KNOW A HALF CAPPUCCINO AND HALF FRAPPUCCINO?
OKAY
ONE CRAPPUCCINO!

Betty
By Delainey and Rasmussen
SORRY, BETTY – I GOT SO WRAPPED UP YAPPING ABOUT WHAT MAKES ME TICK THAT I LOST TRACK OF THE TIME
THAT'S OKAY, ALEX, I UNDERSTAND. IT'S THE SAME WITH EVERYONE — WHAT MAKES US TICK IS WHAT MAKES US TALK
Delainey & Rasmussen

GOLF IS THE SPORT FOR ME – I'M LEARNING A LOT ABOUT MYSELF
IT'S EVEN GOT ME READING PHILOSOPHY – LIKE, DO YOU KNOW WHICH PHILOSOPHER SAID...
ACTUALLY, I THINK EVERY PHILOSOPHER SAID THAT – I BELIEVE IT'S THE STARTING POINT FOR EACH NEW PHILOSOPHICAL DISCOURSE
DER

OH, BY THE WAY, I'M THINKING OF BREAST REDUCTION
REALLY?
YEAH, I FIGURE IT'LL HELP MY BACKSWING
DER
WOW! YOU ARE GETTING SERIOUS ABOUT THIS SPORT
YOU'RE DARN TOOTIN'

WHAT'S THEIR PROBLEM?
WHEN YOUR DRIVE ALMOST HITS SOMEBODY, YOU'RE SUPPOSED TO YELL "FORE" TO GIVE THEM A CHANCE TO GET OUT OF THE WAY
OH
SEE, THERE'S ONE MORE THING FROM GOLF THAT I CAN APPLY TO MY EVERYDAY LIFE
?
FORE!
!
!
DER

Betty
BY Delainey & Rasmussen
LET'S GO IN HERE
OPTICAL
THE WINDOWS TO MY SOUL COULD USE REFRAMING
?
MY OPTOMETRIST RECOMMENDS SMALL FRAMES —WHAT DO YOU THINK?
OKAY...
HOW ABOUT THESE?
THESE?
THESE?
THESE?
THESE?
THESE?
YOU BE SURE TO TELL ME IF YOU SEE SOMETHING YOU LIKE. REMEMBER, WITHOUT MY GLASSES ON I'M BLIND AS A BAT
Delainey & Rasmussen

SMALLER AND CLOSER IS BETTER THAN BIGGER AND FURTHER AWAY FROM THE EYES
THERE! WHAT DO YOU THINK OF THOSE?
I THINK THEY LOOK OKAY- THIS IS THE MIRROR, RIGHT?
ACTUALLY, THE MIRROR'S TO YOUR LEFT— THAT'S A PICTURE OF CLAUDIA SCHIFFER
IT'S NO USE. I CAN'T TELL—WITHOUT MY PRESCRIPTION LENSES, I'M BLIND AS A BAT
WELL, I THINK THEY LOOK GREAT!
BUT FOR SOMETHING AS IMPORTANT AS EYEGLASSES, I ALWAYS RECOMMEND A SECOND OPINION
WHY NOT ASK THAT STYLISH YOUNG MAN BEHIND YOU?
EXCUSE ME, WOULD YOU MIND?
I'D BE HAPPY TO - THEY LOOK GREAT
DER
THIS ISN'T WORKING. I CAN'T TELL IF THESE GLASSES ARE RIGHT FOR ME OR NOT, AND NO OFFENSE, BUT I DON'T TRUST YOU
I SEE
WELL, IF YOU WANT AN HONEST, UNBIASED ANSWER, WHY NOT ASK THE PRIEST IN THE CHURCH NEXT DOOR?
DER
FATHER— WELL?
SORRY, ONE OF THE REASONS I'M NOT ALLOWED TO MARRY IS TO SAVE ME FROM ANSWERING QUESTIONS LIKE THAT

THANKS FOR HELPING ME PICK OUT GLASSES
NO PROBLEM
THEY LOOK GOOD ON ME, RIGHT?
OF COURSE
WELL, THEY SHOULD BE READY BY NOW —LET'S GO PICK 'EM UP
LET'S
A LITTLE, UM, ROCOCO, DON'T YOU THINK?
BETTY, THERE'S ONLY SO MUCH A PERSON CAN SAY THROUGH AUSTERITY

IN A FEW MOMENTS, YOUR MOTHER WILL BE HOME WITH NEW GLASSES ON
AS MEN, WE MUST SAY WE LIKE THEM REGARDLESS OF HOW THEY LOOK AND, IF WE DON'T LIKE THEM, NOT ONE FLICKER OF SHOCK, DISAPPROVAL OR MIRTH MUST APPEAR IN OUR EXPRESSIONS
GOT IT
I'M HOME
OKAY, SHE'S HOME. YOU GO IN AND SEE YOUR MOM —I'LL BE IN IN A MOMENT...
AFTER I TAKE A SNEAK PEEK THROUGH THE LIVING ROOM WINDOW

I'M COMING IN TO SHOW YOU MY NEW GLASSES—READY?
YES! READY!
WOW! I THINK THEY LOOK SUPER!
HE LIKED THEM?
YES, HE LOOKED STRAIGHT AT ME AND SAID THEY LOOK SUPER!
SO, WHAT'D YOU USE? EYEDROPS?
AND HOW!

CAN I SEE YOUR NEW GLASSES FOR A SEC?
SURE, DO YOU LIKE THEM?
OOPS
CRUNCH
BUT THEY DIDN'T BREAK. THE FRAMES DIDN'T BEND AND THE LENSES DIDN'T SCRATCH OR CRACK BECAUSE THEY WERE MADE USING SPACE-AGE TECHNOLOGY
ONCE AGAIN I QUESTION THE WHOLE POINT OF PUTTING A MAN ON THE MOON

THEY REALLY ARE SOMETHING!
COME ON, GIVE ME YOUR REAL OPINION. LIKE IN THE MILITARY —I GIVE YOU PERMISSION TO SPEAK FREELY
I HAVE PERMISSION TO SPEAK FREELY, JUST LIKE IN THE MILITARY?
OKAY— HERE'S WHAT I REALLY THINK...
I'LL BET THE SAME THING HAPPENS IN THE MILITARY

The rich, peaty overtones, the smooth hint of sherry in the complex mature nose make this 21-year-old highland single-malt a delight.
MORE ORANGE JUICE?

Betty
By Delainey and Rasmussen.
THIS IS KIND OF NICE, ISN'T IT?
SURE
HOW MUCH?
25¢
HERE, BUY IT
BUY IT? ARE YOU KIDDING? I HAVE TO BARGAIN FIRST
BUT...
NO 'BUTS.' THAT'S HOW IT'S DONE
HOW ABOUT 15¢ FOR THIS?
22¢
16¢
17¢
21¢
18¢
19¢
OKAY, 18¢
HERE YOU GO
I DON'T HAVE ANY CHANGE LEFT—IF YOU WAIT A WHILE...
IT'S ONLY 7¢. DON'T WORRY ABOUT IT
THANKS
Delainey & Rasmussen.
SEE? THAT'S HOW IT'S DONE
I'M NOT SAYING ANYTHING UNTIL I'M BACK ON MY PLANET

Betty
By Delainey and Rasmussen
RESTAURANTE
HEY, LOOK: ONE OF THOSE YEAR-ROUND CHRISTMAS STORES
LET'S CHECK IT OUT
THIS IS WEIRD ISN'T IT?
YEAH
IT'S JUST LIKE WE LEFT SUMMER AND WALKED RIGHT INTO WINTER
YEAH
CHRISTMAS BOUTIQUE
HEY! I LOST MY TAN!

HEY!
SVEN HEAD IS COMING TO TOWN!
SVEN HEAD? THE BLOOD-SPEWING SELF-MUTILATING DEVIL-WORSHIPING LINGERIE-WEARING SHOCK ROCKER??
YEAH
CAN I GO?
YOU SAID YES?!
I WAS TRYING TO ROB THE SHOW OF ITS COUNTERCULTURAL CACHET

I CAN'T BELIEVE YOU'RE ALLOWING OUR SON TO GO SEE THAT DISGUSTING SHOCK ROCKER
GIVE IT A REST
DON'T YOU REMEMBER YOUR TEEN YEARS? WHEN YOUR PARENTS FORBID YOU SOME-THING, DIDN'T IT MAKE YOU WANT TO DO IT ALL THE MORE?
I GUESS SO. SURE
SPEAKING OF WHICH...
GO TO SLEEP, BUSTER

THIS IS SAFFRON. SHE'S GOING TO HELP ME GET READY FOR THE SVEN HEAD CONCERT
GET READY FOR A CONCERT? WHAT'S WRONG WITH JEANS AND A T-SHIRT?
I'M SERIOUS, WHAT'S WRONG WITH JEANS AND A T-SHIRT??

HAVE FUN. I'LL BE RIGHT HERE WHEN THE CONCERT LETS OUT
NIN
YOUR MOM'S COOL
YEAH
I FEEL LIKE I'M GOING TO BE SICK
I H-H-HATE YOU... I WANT TO CUT OFF YOUR FACE!!
I H-H-HATE YOU... I WANT TO CUT OFF YOUR FACE...
TELL ME ABOUT THE SVEN HEAD CONCERT
MOM, IT WAS SO-O-O COOL!
DURING ONE SONG HE EVEN WIPED HIS REAR END WITH THE FLAG AND THREW IT INTO THE CROWD!

Betty
By Delainey and Rasmussen
INEXPLICABLY THE SCHOOL OF BONEFISH DOUBLED BACK
I CAST MY LINE... AHHH! A CONNECTION!
TWO PATHS INTERSECT IN THE THRESHOLD BETWEEN WORLDS
I BASK IN THE BONEFISH'S HEROIC EFFORT TO FREE HIMSELF!
FINALLY IT YIELDS, AND I PAUSE IN AWE OF ITS SILVER, MUSCULAR PERFECTION
WHEN IT RETURNS TO ITS WORLD AND I TO MINE, I AM RENEWED AND GRATEFUL
THAT'S WHAT I WANT TO DO!
GO BONEFISHING IN BISCAYNE BAY?!
WRITE POETRY!
WATCHING THE OUTDOORS NETWORK WITH OUR SON ISN'T HAVING QUITE THE EFFECT I'D HOPED
Delainey & Rasmussen

ONE BIG RALPH HAMBURGER, PLEASE
ACTUALLY WE DON'T CALL THEM HAMBURGERS, WE CALL THEM SANDWICHES
SURE, BUT THEY'RE STILL MADE WITH HAMBURGER, AREN'T THEY? AREN'T THEY?
YOU WANT FRIES WITH THAT?
FRIED WHAT?

WHAT'S THE ASSIGNMENT?
QUESTIONS 2-6, 13, 17 AND 22
OKAY
RIGHT
HE STILL HASN'T LEFT US IN THE DUST, HAS HE?
NOPE!

COME INTO THE KITCHEN FOR A SECOND!
CAN'T IT WAIT? THE GAME IS ON
NO, IT CAN'T, I WANT YOU TO SEE ONE OF THOSE FEMININE TOUCHES THAT MAKE A HOUSE A HOME!
LIKE THE ONE ON MY EAR?

MOM, DO WE HAVE A BIBLE?
SURE WE DO
WE'RE STUDYING A SHORT STORY. MY TEACHER SUGGESTED WE READ A FEW PAGES FROM THE BIBLE TO HELP US UNDERSTAND IT
OH
HERE YOU GO, OUR FAMILY BIBLE. MY MOTHER GAVE IT TO ME WHEN I GOT MARRIED. IT WAS HERS BEFORE THAT
IT'S STILL IN THE PLASTIC WRAP
OUR FAMILY'S NEVER BEEN VERY CHURCHY

HOW DO YOU FIND THE BIBLE?
IT'S NOT LIKE ANY BOOK I'VE EVER READ BEFORE
HOW SO?
THE PAGES ARE ALL SKINNY, THERE'S GOLD SHINY STUFF ON THE EDGES OF 'EM, AND THE COVER IS HARD, YET BENDY
I SHOULDN'T BE RELIEVED, BUT I AM

GOOMF!

SPOT THE BIBLE READER
MAN-O-MAN, DID HE EVER CONNECT ON THAT PITCH!
HOMER!
WELL SMOTE!

MOM, CAN I ASK YOU A QUESTION?
SURE
WAS I BAPTIZED?
UM, WELL...
ACTUALLY, NO, YOU WEREN'T
YOU KNOW HOW SOME PEOPLE DRIVE FORDS, AND SOME PEOPLE DRIVE CHEVYS, AND OTHER PEOPLE DRIVE FOREIGN CARS? WELL, WE WANTED YOU TO BE ABLE TO MAKE UP YOUR OWN MIND ABOUT WHAT KIND OF CAR YOU DRIVE
AND?
HE'S PICKED HIS CAR

SO WHAT DO WE DO ABOUT THIS?
WELL, THERE'S A TON OF CHURCHES IN THE YELLOW PAGES
I GUESS WE PICK ONE AND SEE IF THEY DO BAPTISMS
LET'S SEE THERE'S THE "AAAAAAAAAAAARDVARK HOUSE OF CHRISTIAN WORSHIP,"... THE "AAAAAAAH GOSPEL TEMPLE"... THE "AAAAAAAMEN ALLIANCE TABERNACLE!"...
WOW! THERE MUST BE A LOT OF COMPETITION IN THE RELIGION TRADE
IT'S A GOD-EAT-GOD BUSINESS

YES, BAPTISM FOR OUR SON, SURE... THAT'S FINE... 'BYE
IT'S SET. WE HAVE AN APPOINTMENT TO MEET FATHER BILL
OKAY
ARE YOU NERVOUS?
NO- WHY SHOULD I BE NERVOUS?
STILL TIME TO TURN BACK
NOTICE HOW YOU ALWAYS HAVE TO WALK UP INTO A CHURCH — I HAVEN'T EVEN SET FOOT IN IT AND IT'S ALREADY MESSING WITH MY MIND
DER

HERE WE GO... TAKE A DEEP BREATH
!
!
HELLO, I'VE BEEN EXPECTING YOU...
WHAT?
DER
OH, SILLY ME. I'M STANDING IN FRONT OF THAT SHINY, CIRCULAR PLAQUE AGAIN, AREN'T I?

WELL, THAT'S THAT
YES, IT WASN'T AS BAD AS I EXPECTED
ALL WE HAVE TO DO IS FIND SOME-ONE TO STAND AS GODPARENT
YEAH
WE MUST KNOW SOMEBODY...
ANYONE COME TO MIND?
UM, I'M THINKING..
DER
STILL THINKING?
YEP

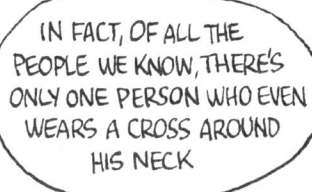

Panel 1: THIS IS PRETTY PATHETIC, BUT NOBODY WE KNOW IS RELIGIOUS AT ALL / I KNOW

Panel 2: IN FACT, OF ALL THE PEOPLE WE KNOW, THERE'S ONLY ONE PERSON WHO EVEN WEARS A CROSS AROUND HIS NECK / ARE YOU SAYING WE SHOULD ASK HIM?

Panel 3: DEX? MY BROTHER? GODPARENT TO OUR SON? / WHAT CHOICE DO WE HAVE?

Panel 4: I SAY AGAIN, HIM? / ASK HIM

Panel 5: YES, I WOULD BE HONORED AND DELIGHTED TO BE YOUR SON'S GODFATHER

Panel 6: SEND THE LAD OVER ANYTIME AND I'LL START HIM ON HIS RELIGIOUS EDUCATION

Panel 7: I'M CURIOUS. I SAY WE DO IT

Panel 8: OKAY, NOW KISS THE DICE AND SAY, "PLEASE, GOD, A SEVEN!"

Panel 9: SEE, ARTHUR JR., IN MY VIEW, WE ARE ALL PUT HERE FOR A REASON

Panel 10: WE'RE ALL PART OF A GRAND PLAN—

Panel 11: —FIFTY ON THE FIVE TO WIN IN THE SEVENTH AT AQUEDUCT—

Panel 12: REVEALED TO US ONE HORSE AT A TIME

YOUR HORSE CAME LAST
YEP
THAT'S HOW IT IS SOMETIMES
SOMETIMES YOU LOSE, SOMETIMES YOU WIN
I SEE. SO IT BALANCES OUT
DER
ACTUALLY, NO. YOU LOSE WAY MORE THAN YOU WIN. WHEN YOU WIN BIG, YOU'LL LOSE EVEN BIGGER
AND THAT'S YOUR RELIGION?
NO- THE RELIGION PART COMES LATER- WHEN YOU CAN'T PAY THE 'VIG'
IT DOESN'T BUG YOU WHEN YOU LOSE MONEY?
NOPE, IT'S JUST THE COST OF PLAYING THE GAME
AND PLAYING THE GAME IS WHAT ADDS SPICE TO LIFE
WELL, WELL, WHO DO I SEE BUT DEXY... DO YOU HAVE MY MONEY, DEXY?
DER
OF COURSE, THE SPICE FREQUENTLY TURNS OUT TO BE MEAT TENDERIZER
FOR WEEKS ALL HE DID WAS READ THE BIBLE - NOW IT'S "AINSLIE'S COMPLETE GUIDE TO THOROUGHBRED RACING"
YEP
THAT'S JUST HOW BOYS ARE - THEY'RE NATURALLY CURIOUS ABOUT THINGS
DER
THANKS. THAT EXPLAINS A LOT
HEY, LOOK! RESTORING BUTTERCHURNS!

Betty
By Delainey and Rasmussen
4:00
4:15
4:20
USING THE LOAFMASTER AT NIGHT IS A BAD IDEA
NO KIDDING
Delainey & Rasmussen

YES, IT'S NICE, BUT WHAT ELSE DOES IT DO?
IT'S A WATCH. IT TELLS TIME
I CAN SEE THAT, BUT WHAT ELSE DOES IT DO?
IT JUST TELLS THE TIME
REALLY?
OH
YOU'RE SERIOUS?
I'M VERY DISAPPOINTED IN THE SWISS ARMY WATCHES

ALEX, WHERE'S YOUR UMBRELLA? THERE'S A 90% CHANCE OF RAIN
NOT TO WORRY!
WITH A FEW ZIPS AND TUCKS MY NEW ATTRACTIVE NYLON PURSE THAT CARRIES OVER TEN POUNDS OF ESSENTIALS TURNS INTO AN EQUALLY ATTRACTIVE WET-WEATHER RAIN SLICKER
I GUESS I DIDN'T THINK THIS ONE THROUGH

DRIVE THRU
IT'S NOT JUST STOCK TIPS YOU HAVE TO BE WARY OF ON THE INTERNET

96

Betty
By Delainey and Rasmussen.
OH. I MADE YOU GUYS SANDWICHES AND BEVERAGES, TOO. THEY'RE ON THE KITCHEN COUNTER
ALFRED HITCHCOCK ISN'T THE ONLY MASTER OF SUSPENSE
Delainey & Rasmussen

Betty
By Delainey and Rasmussen.
I WANT TO TRY SOMETHING I'VE READ...
THE THINKING IS THAT A PERSON CAN, BY PICTURING A CONTROL PANEL FOR ANY OF THEIR MENTAL OR PHYSICAL PROCESSES, USE IT TO ADJUST THOSE PROCESSES
IT'S SIMPLE, REALLY. ALL IT IS, IS TAKING CONSCIOUS CONTROL OF THINGS YOU SUBCONSCIOUSLY CONTROL ANYWAY
SO, IF YOU DON'T MIND, I'M GOING TO GIVE IT A TRY BEFORE WE ORDER
GO AHEAD. I'LL TRY IT TOO
METABOLISM
SLOW
MEDIUM
FAST
ABILITY TO KEEP MOUTH SHUT WHILE LISTENING TO CLAPTRAP
MUMS THE WORD
VERY GOOD
GOOD
Delainey & Rasmussen

IF I WEREN'T SO SELF-CONSCIOUS, I COULD WEAR THAT
BETTY! I SAID 'SELF-CONSCIOUS'!..
...NOT 'FAT'! I HEARD! CONGRATULATIONS! YOU'RE ONE RUNG UP THE LADDER OF ACCEPTANCE!

SO, ONCE I SHAKE MY SELF-CONSCIOUSNESS, I'LL BE HAPPY!
THINK SO?
SURE, ONLY UNSELF-CONSCIOUS PEOPLE ARE FREE AND ONLY FREE PEOPLE ARE HAPPY
OF COURSE I DON'T EVER WANT TO GET THAT HAPPY

BETTY! I BOUGHT YOU THIS HAT!
ER..UM, IT'S NICE, UM, THANKS, I THINK
PUT IT ON
OKAY, I'LL COME CLEAN, IT'S PART OF MY THERAPY TO BE LESS SELF-CONSCIOUS
ALEX, IF YOU WANT TO WORK ON BEING LESS SELF-CONSCIOUS, SHOULDN'T YOU BE WEARING THE HAT?
NO, BEING SEEN WITH YOU IN IT IS ENOUGH

100

LOOK WHAT I'VE GOT! EVERYBODY'S FAVORITE MOVIE! THE WIZARD OF OZ!
GREAT!
WHAT?
YOU'VE SEEN IT, HAVEN'T YOU?
OH, SURE, PLENTY OF TIMES, PUT IT ON!
"FOLLOW THE YELLOW..."
SUBMARINE?

YOU SAY YOU'VE SEEN *THE WIZARD OF OZ* AND I SAY "FOLLOW THE YELLOW..." AND YOU SAY "SUBMARINE"?
WHAT'S WRONG?
NOT ONLY IS IT WRONG, BUT... TRY THIS— "JOHN, PAUL, GEORGE AND...?"
KRAMER?
KRAMER?
NO?
JOHN, ARE YOU COMPLETELY IGNORANT OF POPULAR CULTURE?
NOT ENTIRELY. ASK ME ABOUT THE NOVELS OF WILLIAM SHATNER

I'M SPEECHLESS! ...YOU'VE NEVER SEEN THE WIZARD OF OZ?
AS A KID, I WASN'T BIG ON POPULAR ENTERTAINMENT
PREPARE TO BE DELIGHTED!
"DELIGHTED," JOHN, DOES NOT MEAN "LIGHTS OUT"
LIONS AND TIGERS AND BEARS, OH, MY!

WELL, THERE YOU HAVE IT! THE WIZARD OF OZ! WHAT DO YOU THINK?
I CAN CERTAINLY SEE WHY YOU LOVE IT SO MUCH
CAN'T YOU JUST!
SURE, IT'S OBVIOUS. IT'S AS IF IT WAS TAILOR-MADE FOR YOU
YES, YES, IT IS
IT'S ABOUT ONE WOMAN WHO COVETS ANOTHER WOMAN'S SHOES
IT'S ABOUT— WHAT?
DER

JOHN AND I WATCHED THE WIZARD OF OZ LAST NIGHT
UH-OH
"UH-OH"—YOU GOT THAT RIGHT!
HE COMPLETELY MISSED THE POINT OF THE MOVIE
HE THOUGHT IT WAS ABOUT ONE WOMAN COVETING ANOTHER WOMAN'S SHOES!
WHEN IT'S REALLY ABOUT HOW ALL WOMEN ARE POWERFUL AND ALL MEN ARE FLAWED
THEY ONLY SEE WHAT THEY WANT TO SEE

DER
DARLING, CHECK THIS OUT!
I'M DONE!
IT'S OUR OWN WEBSITE! ALL HOOKED UP AND READY FOR HITS FROM FAMILY AND FRIENDS
IS THAT A PICTURE OF ME IN A BATHING SUIT?
YEAH, I TOOK IT OUT OF OUR ALBUM AND SCANNED IT
...AND THEN WHAT HAPPENED?
JOHN GOT HIS FIRST HIT FROM FAMILY A LOT SOONER THAN EXPECTED

SOMEONE ACCESSES OUR WEB PAGE – THEY SEE THIS SCREEN AND THESE ICONS
THEN, DEPENDING ON THEIR INTERESTS, THEY COULD CLICK ON, SAY, "LAST YEAR'S VACATION," "FAMILY NEWSLETTER," "PHOTO GALLERY" OR "FAVORITE LINKS"
WHAT?
HONESTLY? YOU'RE NOT THRILLED TO BE PART OF CYBERSPACE?
DID YOU SAY CYBERSPACE OR CYBURBIA?

WHAT'S THAT?
ALEX AND JOHN'S WEB PAGE
ALEX AND JOHN HAVE THEIR OWN WEB PAGE?
MAN!
"WEB PAGE DESIGN FOR DOLTS"?
WE CAN'T JUST KEEP UP WITH THE JONESES' STUFF ANYMORE WE ALSO HAVE TO KEEP UP WITH THEIR VIRTUAL STUFF

I'VE DONE IT! COME SEE!
WE NOW HAVE OUR OWN WEB PAGE, TOO!
SEE! NOW ALL WE HAVE TO DO IS FILL IT WITH 'CONTENT'
OKAY, HOW ABOUT THIS?..."FAMILY GETS WEBSITE, DISCOVERS LIFE EMPTY"
HMM... PUNCHY... GOOD HUMAN INTEREST ANGLE – I SAY RUN IT!

Betty
By Delainey and Rasmussen
15% OFF
CAN WE GET OUT OF HERE?
THE NEXT TIME WE HAVE A MOVIE/SHOPPING DAY, LET'S NOT GO SEE A 'SLASHER' FILM
Delainey and Rasmussen

YOU'RE WATCHING SOME WOMAN ON A COUCH?
YEAH
IT'S FASCINATING. SHE'S INSTALLED A VIDEO CAMERA IN HER APARTMENT THAT BROADCASTS HER LIFE OVER THE INTERNET LIVE, 24 HOURS A DAY
THE REALITY OF IT IS RIVETING... LOOK! SHE'S SHIFTING POSITION...
WHAT ARE YOU DOING?
WATCHING YOU WATCH HER. YOU LIKE REALITY; I LIKE ABSURDITY

YOU STILL WATCHING THAT GIRL'S LIVE APARTMENT WEBSITE CAMERA?
YEAH
WHERE IS SHE? IN THE BATHROOM?
SHE'S GONE OUT
SO YOU'RE WATCHING AN EMPTY ROOM?
YES, THE STILLNESS, THE QUIET... IT'S ALL SO INTEREST-ING
BUT SHE'LL BE BACK IN A FEW MINUTES, IF YOU WANT TO STICK AROUND —I THINK SHE WENT FOR MILK
I WAS, BUT SEEING AS HOW YOU JUST GAVE AWAY THE PLOT...

STILL WATCHING THAT GIRL'S INTERNET APARTMENT CAMERA?
YEAH, SHE'S READING A MAGAZINE. AN HOUR AGO SHE MADE A PHONE CALL
YOU KNOW, UNTIL YOU SEE SOMETHING LIKE THIS, YOU DON'T REALIZE HOW MUCH OF OUR LIVES WE SPEND ON SILLY, POINTLESS STUFF!

WHAT'S THAT YOU JUST TYPED?
:)
OH, WAIT! I SEE, YOU'VE MADE A LITTLE SMILEY FACE!
YOU'D BE AMAZED AT WHAT CAN BE DONE WITH KEYBOARD CHARACTERS
CRICK
OH NO!
CAN YOU MAKE A FACE LIKE THIS ONE?

WAS DAD DOING HIS AIR-GUITAR THING AGAIN?
NO, BUT GO ASK HIM YOURSELF
HA!
THANKS. HURT AS I AM, I APPRECIATE THAT I'M STILL ABLE TO SPREAD SUNSHINE
I'M DOWN HERE

TICK TICK
TO SHOW YOU THERE'S NO HARD FEELINGS, I'VE LEFT YOU ONE OF THOSE 'EMOTICON' THINGS ON THE COMPUTER?
CRICK!
"@>-+-+--"?
A ROSE

Betty
By Delainey and Rasmussen

WOW!

YEAH

I'VE NEVER WORN FUR, HAVE YOU?

NOPE

TOO BAD ABOUT FUR. I'LL BET IT FEELS WONDERFUL TO WEAR A COAT LIKE THAT

YEAH

USED TO BE WHEN A MAN GOT SOME EXTRA MONEY HE'D BUY HIS WIFE ONE OF THOSE

YEAH

NOW THEY DON'T

YEAH

I WONDER WHAT THEY'RE SPENDING THEIR EXTRA MONEY ON?

SOLD

Betty
By DeLainey and Rasmussen

I CAN'T SHAKE THE FEELING THAT THE FISH IS MOCKING ME

MAYBE IF YOU TOOK SMALLER BITES AND CHEWED LONGER...

109

VMMM
DAD, HAVE WE BECOME WHAT USED TO BE CALLED 'LIBERATED' MEN?
YES, IF BY 'LIBERATED' MEN YOU MEAN 'SLAVES'

I'M EXHAUSTED, BUT IT FEELS GOOD
YEAH. WE DID IT. WE CLEANED THE WHOLE HOUSE
IT'D BE NICE IF WE COULD THINK OF A WAY TO AVOID HAVING TO DO IT AGAIN UNTIL YOUR MOM'S BACK ON HER FEET
YEAH
G'NIGHT, DAD
G'NIGHT, SON

DO ME A FAVOR. LOOK UP BACK SPASMS ON THE INTERNET AND TELL ME WHAT YOU FIND
SURE, MOM
BACK+SPASMS
SEARCH
WELL?
WHAT CAME UP WERE PLENTY OF BACKS, LOTS OF FRONTS AND SOME OF WHAT MIGHT BE CALLED SPASMS

Panel 1:
- How's the back?
- The slightest movement is still excruciating agony

Panel 2:
- Any chance you could join us downstairs for a video?
- I'm afraid not

Panel 3:
- Steven Seagal it is

Panel 4-7 (middle row):
- Slurp!
- How's the soup, Dad?
- It's perfect! Good enough to eat but not good enough that your mother will ask us to do it again when she's back on her feet

Panel 8:
- HA HA HA HA!
- What's so funny?

Panel 9:
- This Robotman cartoon! In it Monty has a sore back like you do, except he gets acupuncture — with hilarious consequences!
- HA HA HA HA

Panel 10:
- Wisdom cares not where you find it

SHE'S HOME
HOW'D IT GO?
FINE! MY BACK FEELS GREAT
URK!
I THINK THEY LEFT ONE IN BY MISTAKE
FLOP!
OH, COME ON, YOU TWO! YOU'VE GOT TO EXPECT THAT SORT OF JOKE FROM SOMEBODY WHO'S JUST COME FROM AN ACUPUNCTURIST!

LOOKS LIKE YOU GUYS DID A GREAT JOB KEEPING THE HOUSE WHILE I WAS RECOVERING
ALL WE DID WAS APPLY OUR NATURAL TALENTS IN UNDERSTANDING SPATIAL RELATIONSHIPS, MECHANICAL REASONING AND LOGISTICAL THINKING AND IT WAS A PIECE OF CAKE
WHICH EXPLAINS THE KNIFE IN THE PEANUT BUTTER JAR?
ONE OF OUR MANY INNOVATIONS, YES

IT'S NICE TO GET OUT WITH YOU ON A SATURDAY MORNING
I KNOW
NORMALLY IT'S THE TIME I CATCH UP ON MY HOUSEWORK, BUT UNTIL MY BACK GETS BETTER... MY HUSBAND AND SON ARE DOING IT
IS THAT BACK OF YOURS EVER GOING TO HEAL?
NOT IF I KNOW WHAT'S GOOD FOR ME

Betty
By Delainey and Rasmussen.
YOU'VE GOT TO LOVE THESE NEW-STYLE COFFEE PLACES
YOU SAID IT. I'M UP ENOUGH FOR A REFILL AND A CROISSANDWICH!
Delainey & Rasmussen

Betty
By Delainey and Rasmussen
THERE'S SOMETHING VERY FAMILIAR ABOUT THIS
GODZILLA? SURE, IT'S A REMAKE
BOOM
BASH!
CLANG!
ARRGH
NO, THAT'S NOT IT...
WELL, IT'S A GIANT MONSTER IN NEW YORK MOVIE, LIKE KING KONG...
NO, THAT'S NOT IT, EITHER
WELL, IT'S PART OF A POPULAR GENRE OF MOVIES WHICH INCLUDES WESTERNS, WHERE AN OUTSIDER ARRIVES AND SHOOTS UP THE TOWN...
ACTUALLY, IT MIGHT NOT BE A MOVIE AT ALL
?
DON'T WORRY, IT'LL COME TO ME...
LATER
ARRRGH!
BUMP!
BASH!
WHERE ARE MY @#!!*CAR KEYS?
CLANG!
SNAP
I'VE GOT IT!
GODZILLA
Delainey & Rasmussen

115

!
BETTY! LOOK!
POWDER STICKS! RED HOTS! LICORICE PIPES! SEA FOAM! GUMBALLS! CARAMELS! JAWBREAKERS! WOW!
I HAVEN'T SEEN THIS STUFF SINCE I WAS A KID!
SHOULD I OR SHOULDN'T I?
YOU SHOULD!
BETTY, AREN'T YOU SUPPOSED TO ACT AS MY CONSCIENCE IN MATTERS LIKE THIS?
I WAS GOING TO, RIGHT UP UNTIL I SAW THE CRACKER JACKS

BOOKSIGNING
"NO MORE PERFECTIONISM"
SKRIT
DANG!
NEW BOOK, PLEASE

HOW ABOUT MEATLOAF FOR SUPPER TONIGHT?
THAT SOUNDS AWFUL!
"AWFUL"?
I MEANT TO SAY "AWESOME"! MEATLOAF WOULD BE "AWESOME"
YOU MEANT TO SAY "AWESOME," BUT WHAT YOU WERE THINKING WAS "AWFUL". IT'S A CLASSIC FREUDIAN SLIP. I'LL TELL YOU WHAT, WHY DON'T YOU FEND FOR YOURSELF TONIGHT?
IF FREUD WERE ALIVE TODAY, MY GUESS IS HE'D BE EATING A LOT OF NACHOS

OOOF!
BY THE WAY, MY AEROBICS INSTRUCTOR HAS INCORPORATED SOME MARTIAL ARTS MOVES INTO OUR ROUTINES

YOU'RE REALLY DOING MARTIAL ARTS IN YOUR EXERCISE CLASS?
YEP
WE RUN ON THE SPOT... THEN JAB! JAB! JAB!
UPPERCUT! UPPERCUT!
CROSS! CROSS!
PALM STRIKE! PALM STRIKE!
AEROBICS HAS LOST ITS INNOCENCE

HEY! "THE SHINING"! THESE MEGA-BOOKSTORES HAVE EVERY-THING!
REMEMBER THE MAZE? HOW CREEPY THAT WAS IN THE MOVIE?!
DOI! EVER SINCE I'VE HAD A FEAR OF MAZES!
ME TOO!
!
!

Betty
By Delainey and Rasmussen.
PUFF PUFF PUFF PUFF
PUFF PUFF PUFF PUFF
PUFF PUFF PUFF PUFF
PUFF PUFF PUFF
PUFF PUFF PUFF
PUFF PUFF PUFF
I'VE GIVEN UP THE IDEA OF MY BODY BECOMING BEAUTIFUL — NOW I JUST WANT IT TO SUFFER
Delainey & Rasmussen.

WELL, I MIGHT AS WELL GET STARTED
SPLAT!
HEY, MY OLD HARD HAT!
IF YOU DON'T MIND, I'M NOT IN THE MOOD FOR IRONY AT THE MOMENT

WOW, MY OLD HARD HAT
FOR YEARS I PRACTICALLY LIVED IN THIS THING
REMEMBER ME? I'M THE MAN YOU MARRIED
SURE, GO AHEAD RUB IT IN

THAT SETTLES IT. I'M A JOKE
TODAY I FINALLY DECIDED TO CLEAN OUT THE UPSTAIRS CLOSET. I STARTED —THEN I FOUND THIS
IT'S MY OLD JOURNAL. THE LAST ENTRY WAS FIVE YEARS AGO
"TOMORROW I'M GOING TO CLEAN OUT THE UPSTAIRS CLOSET"
NEVER LEAVE A PAPER TRAIL OF YOUR GOOD INTENTIONS

Betty
By Delainey and Rasmussen.
I'M DONATING YOUR OLD CRUTCHES TO THE SALVATION ARMY
!
BUT I MIGHT NEED THOSE AGAIN. I DID WHEN I TWISTED MY ANKLE THAT TIME
OH THAT'S RIGHT. THAT'S WHEN YOU WERE PLAYING SOCCER
AND REMEMBER WHEN I SPRAINED THE OTHER ANKLE?
RIGHT. PLAYING BALL HOCKEY
THAT'S RIGHT
BUT WHEN WAS THE LAST TIME YOU DID ANY OF THAT STUFF?
HEY, LONG TIME NO SEE. WHAT BRINGS YOU BACK?
MY WIFE WAS THROWING OUT MY CRUTCHES

LET ME GUESS, YOU WERE ONE OF THOSE HORSE-CRAZY GIRLS WHEN YOU WERE LITTLE
YEP
WHAT IS IT ABOUT GIRLS AND HORSES ANYWAY?
DON'T THINK OF THEM AS HORSES
THINK OF THEM AS LARGE BRUTES TO BEND TO OUR WILL
LET'S GO INTO THAT SHOE STORE

HERE!
?
IT'S THE HORSE FROM THE JUNK STORE WINDOW!
DO YOU LIKE IT?
I'M TOUCHED! THAT'S SO SWEET OF YOU!
"SWEET"? AS IN WELL-MEANING BUT MISGUIDED?
WOULD YOU PREFER "DARLING"?

THAT HORSE STATUE I BOUGHT YOU ISN'T COOL, IS IT?
SURE IT IS
AND I VALUE IT AS A GIFT. IT'S JUST THAT I DON'T NEED TO HAVE THINGS THAT REMIND ME OF MY GIRLHOOD PASSIONS
CAN YOU UNDERSTAND THAT?
NO, NOT REALLY
ORR
4

HEY! BETTY! WHAT DO YOU THINK?
THE THONG!
SO?
THEY SAY WOMEN WHO WEAR THEM ARE MORE CONFIDENT AND THEREFORE MORE SUCCESSFUL
SO THE QUESTION IS, DO YOU WANT TO GET TO THE TOP?
AND THE WAY TO THE TOP STARTS AT THE BOTTOM?

BETTY AND ALEX ARE WEARING 'THONG' UNDERWEAR FOR THE FIRST TIME
SO, HOW DO YOU FEEL?
WEIRD
DO YOU FEEL THE CONFIDENCE THAT THE ARTICLE YOU READ SAID YOU'D FEEL?
DO YOU?
TAKE A LOOK AT ME. WHAT DO YOU THINK?
YEAH, ME TOO

THIS IS MY FIRST AND LAST DAY WEARING THONG UNDERWEAR
I HAVEN'T FELT THE CONFIDENCE YOUR MAGAZINE SAID I'D FEEL
I CAN'T SEE HOW IT CAN HAVE ANY BEARING ON WHETHER I'M SUCCESSFUL OR NOT
ALL I'VE THOUGHT ABOUT ALL DAY WAS COVERING MY BEHIND
BINGO!

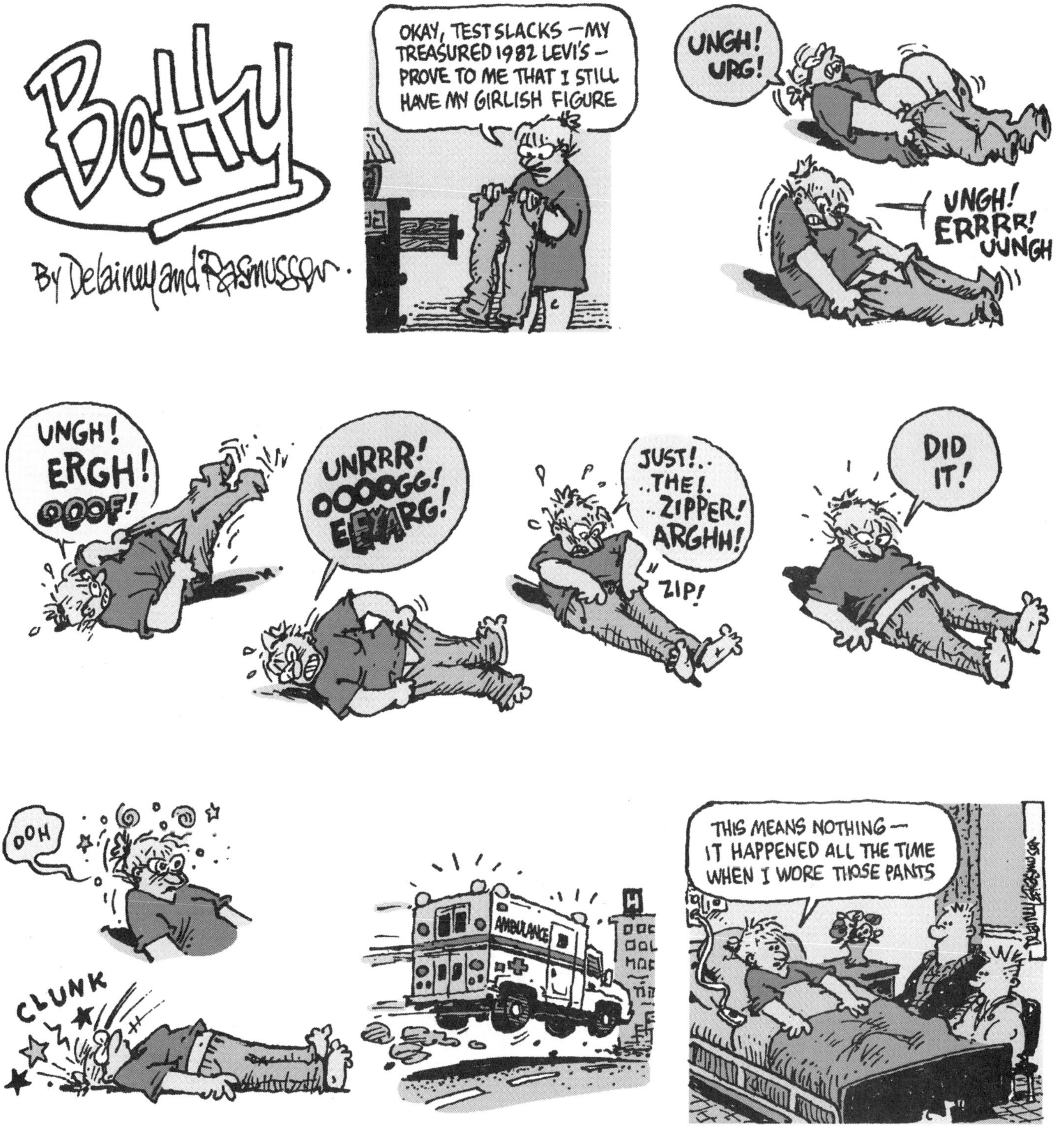
Betty
By Delainey and Rasmussen
OKAY, TEST SLACKS —MY TREASURED 1982 LEVI'S — PROVE TO ME THAT I STILL HAVE MY GIRLISH FIGURE
UNGH! URG!
UNGH! ERRRR! UUNGH
UNGH! ERGH! OOOF!
UNRRR! OOOOGG!
JUST!.. ..THE!. ..ZIPPER! ARGHH!
ZIP!
DID IT!
OOH
CLUNK
AMBULANCE
H
THIS MEANS NOTHING — IT HAPPENED ALL THE TIME WHEN I WORE THOSE PANTS

I PHONED A PSYCHIC HOTLINE
HOW WAS IT?
IT TOTALLY FREAKED ME OUT
BETTY, THIS GIRL ANSWERED THE PHONE AND **SHE KNEW** MY **NAME!** I *HUNG UP RIGHT AWAY!*
ALEX, THEY PROBABLY HAVE CALL DISPLAY
BUT WHAT IF THEY DON'T?

TICK-TOCK
AND THEN-
TICK-TOCK!
TICK-TOCK!
COULD WE CHANGE THE SUBJECT AND TALK ABOUT MY FERTILITY PROBLEMS?— MY BIOLOGICAL CLOCK IS RATHER NOTICEABLE TODAY
NO KIDDING!

BY THE WAY, WHAT DO YOU WANT FOR CHRISTMAS?
WHATEVER
THERE ARE THINGS I NEED, BUT THERE'S NOTHING I REALLY WANT
HOW ABOUT YOU?
THE SAME
AND YOU NEED?
A PEARL NECKLACE
A GOLD WATCH. *YOU?*

Betty
By Delainey and Rasmussen
HO HA HO HA HO HA HO
HA HO HA HO HA HO HA
HO HA HO HA
HA HO HA HO
OKAY, I SEE NOW WHY IT WASN'T SUCH A GOOD IDEA TO PUT A MOTION-SENSING "HO-HO" SANTA ALONGSIDE OUR SOUND-SENSITIVE JIGGLING "HA-HA" CHRISTMAS TREE
MERRY CHRISTMAS
Delainey & Rasmussen

WHAT'S WRONG?
THERE'S ONLY FOUR SHOPPING DAYS LEFT UNTIL CHRISTMAS, AND I STILL HAVEN'T FOUND A PRESENT FOR SAFFRON
GO TELL YOUR FATHER. HE HAS YEARS OF GIFT-BUYING EXPERIENCE UNDER HIS BELT, MAYBE HE CAN HELP YOU
OKAY, I WILL
DAD... THERE'S ONLY FOUR SHOPPING DAYS UNTIL CHRISTMAS AND...
HE SAID "OMIGOSH!" AND ROARED OFF IN OUR CAR TOWARD THE MALL

HEY! MAKING PAPER SNOWFLAKES! I USED TO BE PRETTY GOOD AT THAT!
AS I RECALL, YOU CAREFULLY FOLD A PIECE OF PAPER AND CUT OUT SHAPES FROM IT UNTIL YOU OPEN IT UP TO REVEAL...
WOW!
!
CENSORED
WHAT?

HEY, LOOK! SANTA WAS HERE!
?
?
I MEAN, WHO ELSE WOULD'VE LEFT THE SEAT UP?
HE WAS IN A HURRY. HIS MIND WAS ON OTHER THINGS. HE JUST FORGOT...
Delainey & Rasmussen

Betty
BY Delainey and Rasmussen
SO HOW WAS IT WITH YOUR FAMILY — SANTA CLAUS? KRIS KRINGLE? ST. NICK?
WHEN WE WERE KIDS, IT WAS SANTA CLAUS
BUT AFTER WE STARTED GETTING SHAVERS FOR CHRISTMAS, IT BECAME ST. NICK
EVERY YEAR I LIKE TO FIND AN APPROPRIATE DECORATION FOR THE CHRISTMAS TREE
THE BRIDE AND GROOM WAS FROM THE YEAR WE WERE MARRIED
THE STATUE OF LIBERTY WAS FROM THE YEAR WE VISITED NEW YORK
THE LITTLE ANGEL WAS FOR THE YEAR JUNIOR WAS BORN
THE HOUSE WAS FOR THE YEAR WE BOUGHT THIS CONDO
THE BLENDER WAS FOR THE YEAR WE GOT A BLENDER
THERE SEEMS TO BE RATHER A LOT OF APPLIANCES, BETTY
WHAT CAN I SAY? NOT ALL THE YEARS ARE ACTION-PACKED
Delainey & Rasmussen

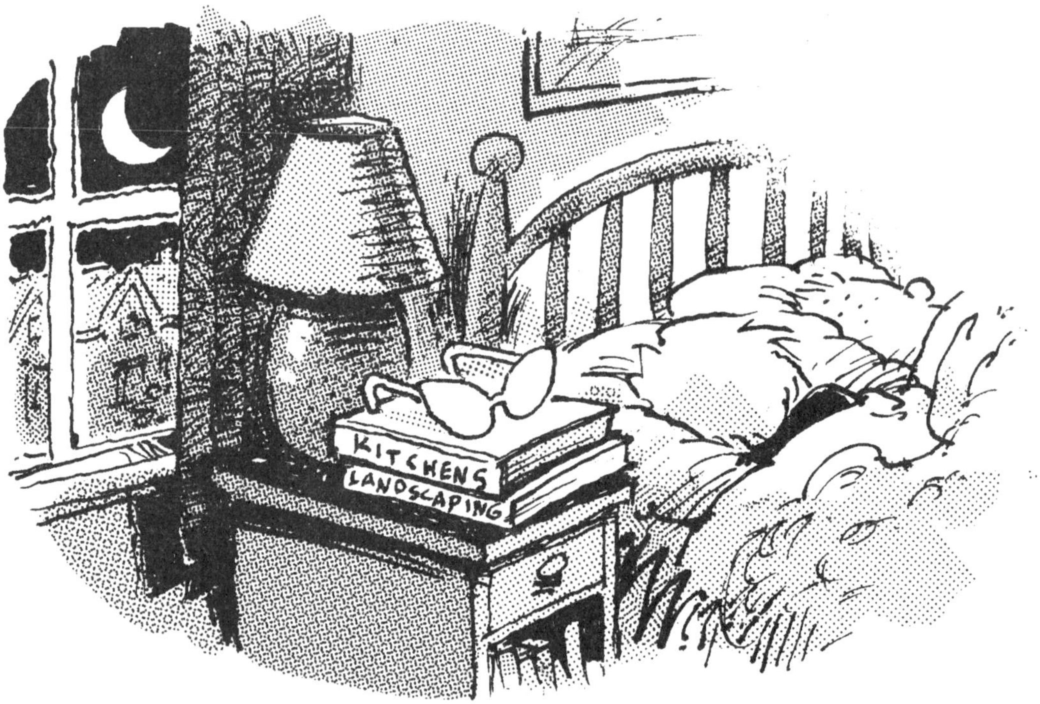
KITCHENS
LANDSCAPING